Fortune's Folly

Fortune's Folly

DEVA FAGAN

Henry Holt and Company

NEW YORK

Henry Holt and Company, LLC
Publishers since 1866
175 Fifth Avenue
New York, New York 10010
www.HenryHoltKids.com

Library of Congress Cataloging-in-Publication Data
Fagan, Deva.
Fortune's folly / Deva Fagan.
p.   cm.
Summary: Ever since her mother died and her father lost his shoemaking
skills, Fortunata has survived by pretending to tell fortunes, but when
she is tricked into telling the fortune of a prince, she is faced with the
impossible task of fulfilling her wild prophecy to save her father's life.
ISBN-13: 978-0-8050-8742-0 / ISBN-10: 0-8050-8742-7
[1. Fairy tales.   2. Prophecies—Fiction.
3. Adventure and adventurers—Fiction.]   I. Title.
PZ8.F165Fo 2009   [Fic]—dc22   2008036780

First Edition—2009
Book designed by April Ward
Printed in the United States of America on acid-free paper. ∞
1   3   5   7   9   10   8   6   4   2

To my husband, Bob,
the magic and the love of my life

Fortune's Folly

CHAPTER

1

L IFE WOULD HAVE BEEN much easier if I believed in fairy tales. I could have set my shoes out on Candlemas Eve and expected the sprites to fill them with candy. I could have dreamed that the Saints would return my poor mother to life. I could have fantasized that some handsome young prince would fall in love with me and carry me off to a life of luxury. Or perhaps I could simply have believed, as my father did, that one day the fairies would return to his workshop, and his shoes would no longer be the ugliest in all the lands.

I could not afford such hopes. I had to deal with reality. "Visconti leatherworks," I called, wedged between the fruit-seller and the wool merchant. "Shoes fit for a noble! Only ten guilders a pair!" Surely someone would buy them at that price.

A long, rolling laugh drowned my next call. I turned to see Captain Niccolo at the nearby textiles booth, watching me as he fondled a length of crimson satin. Red was his color of choice, to match the sash that marked him captain of the guard. Even his tall boots were a bloody scarlet. Father had made them last year, before Mother died, before he had lost his skills. I still remembered how Niccolo had pinched my cheek when he came to collect his purchase and how he'd tried to persuade Father to accept a mere ten guilders. Mother had put a stop to that straightaway, producing the original contract bearing Niccolo's extravagant signature under the price of twenty-five guilders.

"Shoes fit for a noble?" drawled the captain. "Tsk, tsk, Fortunata, those aren't even fit for a festival fool. Your father's name meant something once, but you'll soon wear out even the shred of respect it has left."

"My father is the Master Shoemaker of Valenzia," I said, but I pulled my apron up to cover the basket of hideous shoes I carried. I still held a particularly wretched pair in my other hand.

Niccolo sauntered forward and plucked the red shoes from my grasp. "Dear girl, do you really expect anyone to purchase *these*?" Some of the market-goers had paused to observe our interchange and ogle the shoes. Curse the man, but he was right. Nobody in their right mind would buy them. One stood a full hand span taller than the other. The shorter shoe sprouted a curled toe so extravagant it collapsed under its own weight. The only thing that made the two a pair at all was their vibrant red color, accented by a virulent green that clashed louder than the doge's trumpeters. I swallowed to clear the lump from my throat.

"Perhaps you might try the cathedral hospice," said Niccolo. "There are always a few blind beggars there. Even they wouldn't pay for such horrors, but at least they might be persuaded to *wear* them."

I snatched at the red shoes, but Niccolo jerked them neatly away from my fingers. "You've fallen faster than even I expected." He looked me up and down, taking in the too-short skirts, the too-tight bodice, the dirty ankles. He smirked most broadly at my feet. "Though I see you've still got shoes fit for a noble." I forced myself not to look down at the black-and-yellow boots Father had presented me proudly a few days earlier. I knew quite well I looked like I had two large bumblebees on my feet.

Captain Niccolo leaned close, his voice pitched low. "It's a shame to see a pretty thing like you forced out onto the streets like this. It must be difficult to give up all the luxuries to which you are accustomed. I could provide all that back again, my dear, and more. I could use a pretty maid to serve me. It would not be unpleasant, and you would find me a generous benefactor in all respects."

I met his gaze, but I knew I turned as scarlet as the

cursed shoes. I forced the words out. "I think you mistake me, sir. I doubt my situation could ever be dire enough that I would accept such an offer."

He merely laughed. "You think you have things rough now, Fortunata, but you're only at the barest edge of poverty. When you've spent a winter with nothing but a single cloak, and that pretty face is sunken and pale as a skull, then you'll wish you'd answered differently. You will never sell those shoes for more than a guilder, on my word."

I narrowed my eyes. "On your word? And if I were to meet that challenge?" It was reckless, but Papa and I had eaten nothing but cabbage soup morning, noon, and night for the past week.

"My dear Fortunata, if you can sell those horrors I will buy a pair myself, and wear them to the doge's ball. But you can't be serious."

"I'll have the coin in my purse by the time the noon bell rings," I said, before I could think better of it.

His lips twitched, but he nodded. "I don't gamble unless there's something in it for me. Clearly you have no coin to wager. But I do seem to recall a fine golden chain the doge himself laid upon your father's neck."

"Father's chain of mastery? I could never—"

"If he still deserves it, you need not fear to lose it. Unless you'd rather wager something of your own? My other offer remains open. . . ."

4

I blushed again under his leering smile. "The chain it is. I swear it by the Saints." Silently I sent the Saints an extra prayer that I was not making the biggest mistake of my life.

Niccolo tossed the shoes at me. "Be sure to fetch that gold chain before the noon bell rings. I'm meeting Lady Giaconda for lunch and I plan to wear it. You may find me in Saint Sofia's Square."

I ignored his parting laughter as I scanned the crowds for a target. If the Saints were kind, I would find just the sort of person I was looking for. I passed over the old woman hustling along a flock of children, and the hard-faced man inspecting turnips as if they were gold coins. The quarter bell rang, sending my heart thumping. Saints be with me, I could not lose my father's chain! Perhaps I should have taken the captain's offer.

No, I told myself. I could do this. I had been wheedling sweets out of Zia Rosa since I was a little girl, and I had once convinced miserly Lord Ferdinando to purchase an extra pair of pointed dance shoes when all he wanted was hunting boots. I just needed the right person.

I found him leaning against the side of the pie-seller's stall, one arm wrapped around the post as if it were a woman. He stared mournfully across the street at a gaggle of maids clustered around the ribbon wheels at the booth beside me. I edged closer to the girls, pretending to straighten out my apron as I listened.

After a spate of gossip about the doge's unmarried brother and what color ribbons he might fancy, I had my reward.

"Poor Giacomo the tailor's boy has been staring at us since the quarter bell rang," said one of them. "A shame he's so skinny."

"Better skinny than covered in moles like that smith you favor," said another. "And once he's tailor, he'll have the finest clothes of any tradesman in all Valenzia."

"Are you sweet on him then, Bettina?" said a third girl, with a giggle. "Shall we choose your wedding ribbons?"

Bettina flushed, and that was all I needed to see. Taking a firmer grip on the red shoes, I marched toward the lad Giacomo. As soon as I was within earshot, I took up my cry. "Magic shoes! Find fame and fortune! Bind your true love's heart! Only ten guilders!"

The tailor's boy twisted around, his eyes wide. He really wasn't a bad-looking fellow, with that crop of dark curls and soft, brown eyes. I sidled closer. "You, sir, must have a sweetheart."

"I-I— No, I don't have a sweetheart. That is, there's someone, but she doesn't know—"

"Then I have the shoes for you. With these upon your feet, she will have eyes for no other. Come now, try them on." I pushed him back onto an upturned bucket and had his tattered sandals off a moment later. "See, they are red, like the roses of true love, like the blood of your own passionate heart."

"I don't—" he began, but I had already buckled on the taller shoe. I took up the other, trying surreptitiously to straighten the floppy curling toe. I told myself there was at least a grain of truth in what I was saying. Bettina certainly would have eyes for no other if the lad approached her with these scarlet monstrosities on his feet.

"Are they truly magical?" the boy asked, twitching one foot. The curled toe waggled and toppled over again.

"Of course. Have you never heard of Master Visconti? My father is the Master Shoemaker of all Valenzia, and his own father crafted boots for queens and kings in distant lands." That was also true, for the most part. I never knew my grandfather, but Papa had told me tales of how he traveled the lands plying his trade, and how he had once made a pair of slippers for my grandmother that so impressed the doge of Valenzia that he purchased them himself, right off her feet, to give as a gift to a mighty foreign queen!

"The shoes are fated to be yours," I said, forcing my lips into a smile. "They call out to you—can you not hear them? 'Giacomo,' they cry. 'We are for Giacomo the tailor.'"

"I'm not a tailor," he protested.

"Not yet, but you will be. With the help of these magic shoes." I tightened the last buckle. "There now. Can you not see how special these are? Truly they are unlike any others."

And thank goodness for that! I watched the boy closely. He was weakening. He glanced over to the ribbon booth again. "I haven't much coin."

"The boots are ten guilders," I said. "But for you, for the sake of true love, I will ask only eight."

He gulped. "I have only five."

I had done it. A flush of victory warmed my cheeks, until I saw how tightly he clenched the limp purse that hung from his belt. I knew all too well the pain of giving up even a single coin when one had so little. "Four, then, and use the other to buy your maid a red rose."

As I made my way toward Saint Sofia's Square, the four coins jingled merrily in my pocket. Soon they would be joined by twenty more. I relished the thought of Captain Niccolo's face. And Giacomo the tailor's boy had not suffered too greatly. Bettina had been smiling prettily when I last saw her, standing with the boy, a blossom in her hands. Though I had to admit the girl spent a good amount of time staring at her paramour's bright red feet.

I FOUND THE CAPTAIN beside the fountain of Saint Sofia, offering Lady Giaconda morsels of candied fruits as she simpered and sparkled brighter than the golden Saint's statue in the sun. Niccolo's face fell as he caught sight of me.

"Captain Niccolo," I said, as the noon bell began to chime. I dipped a brief curtsy to Lady Giaconda, who pulled back her skirts and gave a stiff nod. "Your pardon, Lady, but the captain and I have a wager to conclude." I jingled my pocket. "Would you like to try on your new boots, sir?"

His lip curled. "It's not possible. No one could have—"

"By the Saints," said Lady Giaconda. "Do you see those horrible shoes that boy has on?"

I spied Giacomo swaggering along the other side of the square, Bettina on his arm. She didn't even seem to be looking at his shoes anymore.

I turned back to the captain. "You were saying, sir?"

He did not speak. I pulled a pair of boots from my basket and held them out. I could not help but grin. I had chosen for the captain a pair so hideous they had been buried at the very bottom. They looked like giant ruffled sausages, pinker than Lady Giaconda's cheeks, and bore grass-green tassels. In the bright sunlight, they almost glowed. Father had truly outdone himself. Beside them, my bumblebees looked almost pretty.

"Saint Marco preserve me," gasped Lady Giaconda.

"You'll regret this," Niccolo growled, so low only I

could hear it. He snatched the boots from my hand and turned away.

"Excuse me, Captain, but you've forgotten the payment. That will be twenty guilders for the boots. I hope they serve you well at the doge's ball."

"Niccolo, you can't possibly intend to wear those things to the ball," said Lady Giaconda.

"But the captain is a man of his word, Lady," I said. "Don't fear. I'm certain you can find a gown to match. They are a lovely shade of pink, don't you think?"

Niccolo held a handful of gold coins as if he planned to throw them at me. I did not care if I had to pick them from the cobblestones. It was worth it to see him set down, though the fierce look in his eye alarmed me. I wondered if I had pushed things too far.

He shoved the coins at me, and I tucked them away. "Good day, my lady, sir."

"Not yet." The captain seized my wrist. "You have your gold, but I want something in return. If I'm to wear these monstrosities, I'll do it with a gold chain around my neck."

"I wouldn't give you Father's chain if it meant starving in rags. Now let me be or—"

"You'll call for the Guard?" He quirked a black brow at me.

He knew that I knew half the soldiers in Valenzia were in his company, under his command. Soldiers for hire, currently working for the doge, but as like to turn against him if the captain had a better offer. I raised my chin and glared at him with as much fury and as little fear as I could manage. Then I brought my foot down hard on his instep, and the sneering laugh turned into a yelp of pain. My boots might be ugly, but they had nice, hard heels. I twisted free from the captain and darted away. I didn't look back, even when he called out after me, "Stupid girl! You'll regret that. There's nowhere in this town you can hide!"

I could feel the fierce grin on my own lips. It served him right, the slimy scoundrel. I should have known he wouldn't hold to his word. Of course, he did have the strongest force of soldiers in all Valenzia. It had probably not been the wisest thing to do. I was still shaking from the exchange when I reached our hovel of a house. But my mind was burning with a new plan. The captain's threat had given me the idea.

Father and I would leave Valenzia. There was nothing left for us here but Father's name, which had already become a joke. And though I had bested Captain Niccolo this time, I could not count on doing so again. We must seek our fortune elsewhere.

To celebrate, Father and I feasted on a roast chicken with olives that night, with an almond cake from Zia Rosa the sweet-seller for dessert. The next day, with the proceeds from the sausage shoes, I purchased a sturdy cart and a placid gray donkey. We packed Father's supplies neatly into the cart, along with an iron pot, several candles, and what clothes we had left.

"Where will we go?" Father asked. He stared into our empty house. "What if the fairies come back and can't find us?"

I smothered a groan. Before he had lost his gifts, my father had claimed the fairies cleaned his workshop, polishing his tools and sprinkling them with pixie dust so he might craft his marvelous shoes. I knew better. I had caught my mother at it, early one morning. When the fever took her from us, I thought at first it was only grief that had driven away my father's gifts. Then one morning I had found him staring at the row of dusty awls and needles and knives. I offered to clean them myself, but it made no difference. He was convinced the magic was gone.

We were leaving behind the only home I'd ever known, where I had once dreamed a golden life full of promise: dancing at the doge's ball, petal-strewn walks in the gardens, even giggling around the ribbon booth over some lad who was making eyes at me. In this city every corner held some memory of my mother: her favorite bakery, sweet with orange rind and cardamom, the river where she'd taken me as a little girl to sail my toy boat, the bustling markets she'd walked through with such grace and style that people thought her a titled lady.

Now I was leaving all that behind, and all my father could think of was whether the fairies would return? I missed her too, so much that I couldn't even look at our house without blinking back tears, remembering how she'd always waved to me from the kitchen window when I went off running errands. But I was moving on. I was doing the best that I could to keep our life together. Why couldn't he?

"We'll travel to other cities, Papa," I told him, burying my bitterness under a false smile. "Like you did when you were younger, and like Grandpapa did. Surely we'll find plenty of work."

I climbed into the front of the wagon and took the reins. Father stood for a long moment beside the box, looking up at me through his owlish spectacles. "You're so like your mother, Nata," he said at last. "She always knew what to do. I know it's been hard for you this past year. But I promise you, by all the Saints, I'll do everything I can to make you happy. I know I haven't been much of a father."

My throat was tight, seeing him there in his shabby clothing. It was loose on him now; we'd had too many meals of cabbage soup. The silver in his hair caught the morning light, making me realize how old he'd become in the past year. I took his hand and helped him up into the wagon beside me. "You've been working so hard, Papa, I know. But this is our new beginning."

"The fairies will come back, one day," Father murmured. "Such shoes I will make, with their magic."

"We don't need them. We'll do fine on our own. You'll see." I turned my head, brushing the tears from my eyes before he could see them. Then I jiggled the reins and off we went, out through the gates of Valenzia and into the world beyond.

CHAPTER

2

THE FIRST MONTHS after we left Valenzia were particularly difficult. The only bright spot was when I chanced to overhear the rumor that Captain Niccolo had been forced to depart Valenzia, for the murder of the doge's brother and—so the gossips reported—for planning to slay the doge himself. The rogue had been branded with the killer's mark by the Bishop of Valenzia and was to be hanged, but had escaped with the help of his army. I wondered if Father and I should chance returning to Valenzia. But Niccolo had been only a small part of the problem. Father still could not craft a slipper that was anything less than repulsive. I could only hope that one day he might rediscover his lost art.

In time I became used to being cold, to the empty ache of hunger and the boredom of trudging along endless highways in search of work. We could never stay long in any one town. The first patrons gave us business quick enough, but once word got out about the absolute hideousness Father produced, that was the end of that. And sometimes it was worse. We'd been chased out of one hamlet, pelted with the very shoes Father had just crafted. I had a boot-shaped bruise on my backside for weeks afterward.

Humiliation, hunger, and cold were one thing. Even when Father fell ill with a burning fever, I was sure I could minister to him and drive the illness away. I settled him in a cozy hollow along the North Road, certain that he would improve in a day or two and then we could travel on to the next village. But when our donkey was stolen, I gave up hope.

I AWOKE THAT MORNING with a thrill of foreboding. Normally Franca, the donkey, would wake me up. I picketed her near the fire each night, and by the time dawn was gleaming silver on the horizon, she would be nosing me in the back with her big gray head, flicking her tall, velvety ears at me.

But that morning I blinked up at a clear blue sky, the sunlight streaming down over the high green oaks that edged the North Road. Franca never let us sleep this late. She should have been braying like a demon by this time.

I jumped to my feet. "Franca! Franca!" I called. She must have pulled free from the picket and gone off after lusher greenery. I darted around the clearing, peering up and down the road and into the deeper wood. Then suddenly I found myself sprawled forward, my left foot aching from whatever it was I had tripped on. It was the picket spike. I scrambled around to search in the tall grass and came up with the roughly braided cord still tied to the loop of the spike. Dumbly, I stared down at the unraveling end. It had been cut. Franca was gone.

We were, quite literally, at the end of our rope. Without her, we were stuck at the side of the North Road, halfway to nowhere. We had one turnip and a handful of dried noodles. And Papa's fever was not improving.

"Nata . . . what's wrong?" my father mumbled, groping in the grass for his spectacles. His face was flushed, and I could see his hands trembling. He needed an apothecary.

"It's Franca, she's gone. Stolen! Look here, the rope's cut. It's a wonder they didn't slit our throats while they were at it." I gave a bellow of frustration and kicked at the picket.

"Stolen?" he repeated. "What are we to do?"

I bit my lip, looking over at the large cart. Leaving the wagon would mean leaving most of my father's supplies. I began to calculate how much I might be able to carry on my back.

"We could walk," my father said, trying to push himself up. He fell back roughly against the side of the wagon. I sprang forward to catch his free arm as he doubled over in a fit of hacking coughs.

"You're not walking anywhere, Papa," I said. "Don't worry, I'll take care of you. I'll figure out a way." But I could not fathom how. I turned away so that he could not see the tears at the corners of my eyes. This was it. I had tried to take care of Father, like Mother always did. But I had failed. I balled my fists, thumping them against my thighs in frustration.

The sound of jingling bells diverted me. Coming down the road was the most unusual sight I had ever seen—well, other than Father's shoes. It was a large wagon with brightly painted sides and a peaked roof, so that it looked like a little moving house. But no house had ever been such a color as this. Its sides were a brilliant peacock blue, trimmed with rich scarlet and mustard yellow, all scrolled and worked with filigrees of gold and silver.

Even the horses were ostentatious, white with scattered black spots and parti-colored manes and tails. There were four all told: Two pulled the wagon, two bore single riders. The men slouched back easily in the saddles; one was even smoking a pipe. One was grizzled, one fresh-faced, but both had the same suspicious eyes, at odds with the festive scarves knotted at their throats. Both watched us as they passed by. I shivered.

"Perhaps they can help us," Father suggested. "I could make shoes for them, in exchange for a horse."

Father's shoes might be less out of place in such company, but in his current state he could barely lift his awl. Still, perhaps the travelers might at least give us a ride into the next city. It wouldn't hurt to ask.

The peacock-blue cart jingled past. Teetering on the narrow seat, looking as if he might crush it at any moment, was a great bear of a man with a flowing beard but not a lick of hair on his shiny head. Gold loops glittered in his ears, and his huge fingers were banded with more of the same. One of those great hands held the reins loosely, the other twirled a wicked-looking dagger. He saw me approaching, the frayed end of the rope still in my hand, and he grinned. He pulled on the reins and gave a whooping cry. The other two riders came to a stop and cantered back.

"Good day," I said.

"Yes, a very good day," he replied. He continued to play with the dagger, tossing it and catching it. "Lost your donkey, have you? Out here, not a village in sight. Bad place to be left." He made a tsking sound. "And the old man ill as well."

I was about to reply when a strident braying from behind the wagon drew my attention.

"Nata, they've got a donkey just like Franca," Father said, tugging at my skirt and trying to pull himself up. "Perhaps they'll trade her." I pushed him back down and hastened to see the truth for myself.

Father was right, or at least partially right. There was a gray donkey tied to the back of the blue wagon. But she wasn't just like Franca. She *was* Franca.

"You stole our donkey!" I thundered, storming back around to the front.

The two riders merely smiled at this, but the big man threw back his head and let out a great booming laugh. He shook the dagger at me. I took a step back, though the motion was chiding, not threatening. Not yet.

"Ah, young miss, you should know better than to accuse an honest tradesman like myself of such a crime. No, that donkey was a gift to us from the Saints."

"You knew we'd lost a donkey. How did you know it wasn't a horse?" I countered. "Unless you were the one who stole it."

The other riders were laughing outright now. "Better watch yourself, Ubaldo," one said, "or the little captain and her mighty army might take the donkey from you."

"I'm very sorry about your donkey, young miss. But *my* donkey was a gift of the Saints. So it was said by Allessandra the All-Knowing, Mistress of Magic, Doyenne of Dreams."

"Hah," I said. "There's no such thing as magic. Easy

enough to predict you'll have a new donkey if you steal it for yourself."

"So you call the All-Knowing Allessandra a deceiver as well?" said a rich, resonant voice. A woman stepped out from the blue wagon, resplendent in glittering robes and headdress.

"Yes," I said, trying to hide my surprise. She stood tall and straight as a cathedral spire. She was not beautiful, but she was striking, her face an elegant construction of dark hollows and bright angles. Her eyes held mine like candles in a dark room. "There's no truth to fortunes. It's all sham and trickery." I jutted my chin out, planting both hands on my hips.

"Then if I were to tell you that your mother is watching you even now, from her place in the hall of the Saints, you would not believe me?"

Father drew a sharp breath, which set off a fit of coughing. I got angrier. How dare she use Mother in this ruse?

"You just guessed that because Papa and I are alone."

"So sad that the fever took so many," Allessandra went on, her voice now soft and velvety. She looked off into the distance, as if into some misty unseen vision. "It must have been difficult to remain in . . ." She squinted. "Ah, yes, I see it clearly, in Valenzia. So many tears, so many memories of happier times."

"Nata! She does know!" Father gasped.

I frowned at him. "Shush, Papa! It's only another guess. We've met plenty of folk who heard about the fever in Valenzia."

"But how did she know we're from Valenzia?" he asked, blinking at Allessandra.

"Ah, the Saints speak to me. They tell me many things, many things," she intoned.

"Hah!" I said. But I was faltering. How *had* she known? We were hundreds of miles from Valenzia now, on the other side of the Valta Mountains. Then I saw it. "There," I said, flinging out my finger to point at the back of the wagon, where a faint sign was burned into the graying wood. "The wagon-maker's guildmark, with the lion of Valenzia." That was what she had been squinting at, not some distant vision.

I thought I saw the faintest of smiles on Allessandra's lips, but when she spoke again it was with the same portentous voice. "Your father, he was a craftsman. Talented, with many rich patrons. You lived well, had fine gowns and scarlet ribbons."

I smoothed the dirty folds of my tattered skirt. "You can tell this dress was fine once, before I had to tear off the ribbons and sell them. And," I said, plucking at a faintly pink splotch at the bodice, "there are even stains where the color ran. That's how you knew the ribbons were red."

"One day," she went on, unruffled, "you will meet a

handsome prince and endure great and dire peril for your love. But you shall live happily ever after."

"Oh, now that's plain ridiculous," I said, snorting. "You've been reading too many fairy tales."

Just then Father started coughing again. I hastened to him. "Oh, Papa," I murmured. I held his shoulders while the spasms racked his thin frame, and the anger that had sustained me faded away.

I turned back to Ubaldo and Allessandra and the two riders. "Please," I said, "my father is ill. You can't just steal our donkey and leave us here. At least take us with you to the next village, to an apothecary."

"Now then, young miss, what sort of businessman would I be if I took on two penniless travelers?" Ubaldo cleaned his fingernails with the dagger, flicking away the dirt casually.

"We're not penniless," I said before I could help myself. I still had the doge's chain secreted away. In fact, it was wound around my waist, under my chemise and gown. Ubaldo's eyes glinted. Was it my imagination, or were they lingering on the faint bump at my waist? I shook off these concerns; I needed to cover up my inadvertent slip. "That is, we can earn our keep. Father is a great shoemaker. His supplies are there, in the wagon. Once he is well again, he can earn whatever is needed to repay the debt."

"I don't care much for promises from sick men,"

Ubaldo said. "Get on back to your wagon. I've wasted enough time on you two. You'd best pray Allessandra's fortune does come true; you could use a prince right about now."

"If you won't trust Father, then give me work. I can earn our keep," I begged. "Truly, I'm quick. I'll learn whatever work you need done."

Ubaldo snorted. He tossed the dagger to one side, and it sank down into the wooden rim of the wagon, where it quivered slightly. "Bah, this is becoming wearisome. Coso, Cristo, if the girl doesn't hold her tongue, take it. We've work to do." He seized the reins, and would have slapped the horses with them. But Allessandra, who had been silent ever since her last prognostication, leaned down to whisper in his ear. I could not hear what she said, but Ubaldo's flushed face relaxed into smugness, and he stroked his thick beard thoughtfully. What was he up to?

"Well, girl, thank the Saints, for this is your lucky day," he said. "I've decided to take pity on you and your wretch of a father. It so happens that the All-Knowing Allessandra is in need of an assistant. I've decided to take you on to help her. You do what she says and be smart about it, or you'll learn how hard it is to sass with a bloody lip. And you do what *I* say, with no back talk, or you'll learn far worse. You got that?"

I nodded. "And you'll take my father as well, and his tools? And find an apothecary?"

"No back talk means no questions!"

Allessandra spoke again, in a lighter, higher tone than the theatrical voice she'd affected earlier. "I will tend to your father, child. He will be in good hands. Now come along, we'll hitch up your . . . the donkey."

Ubaldo shot her a vicious look at the slip, but she ignored it. I bit my tongue. I knew quite well the donkey was Franca, and she was ours by rights. But rights didn't seem to matter out here. Just strength. This was the only way to make certain Father received the help he needed.

I started to get Father into our wagon after we hitched Franca to it once again. Ubaldo bellowed and waved me away. "No! Do you think me a great idiot? You will ride with Allessandra. Coso, you drive their cart." He gestured peremptorily to the older of the two horsemen. The man sprang down, tied his horse to the back, then took my place.

"Never mind," Allessandra murmured, helping me guide Father to the rear of the blue wagon. "I will see to your father. A bit of my tonic, and he'll be better by next Saints' Day. And," she added, "we can begin your training."

"Training? To do what?"

"Why, to be a fortune-teller. To prognosticate. To

consult the spirit voices and part the veil that guards the future."

"But I told you, I don't believe in that. It's all just a bunch of tricks," I said, as we settled Father onto a narrow padded cot along one side of the covered wagon. The interior was a jumble of shimmering cloth and jangling bells, with a great wardrobe filling one corner and a huge chest in the other. Beside the cot sat a set of movable steps, painted the same bright blue as the wagon itself. Allessandra perched herself on these as we started to roll forward.

She was grinning. "Yes, it is a bunch of tricks. And you are going to learn every one."

THUS I BEGAN my career as a swindler and a charlatan. Allessandra quickly became Alle. She was a demanding teacher, but she shielded me from Ubaldo's rages, which thundered through about once a day. And whatever lies and falseness were behind her fortunes, her tonic was all she claimed. After three days, Father was sitting up again and eating heartily of the noodle soup and crusty onion flatbread that Cristo cooked most every night.

We traveled through several villages outside the city of Andino, stopping in each to allow Ubaldo and his company to ply their trade. Coso and Cristo were jongleurs, tossing balls, fruit, bread, even lighted torches from one to the other in complex and dazzling patterns.

Allessandra told fortunes, of course. And Ubaldo swallowed swords and threw daggers. The great chest in the back of the blue wagon was filled with these deadly implements. When I saw the length of the longest sword, I was certain there must be a trick to it, just as there was to Allessandra's prophesying. I watched in fascinated horror, along with the rest of the crowd, as he held his head back, throat bobbing, and slid that long, terrible steel into his mouth.

Bad as that was, it was nowhere near as nerve-racking as watching the dagger throwing. Or rather, *hearing* the dagger throwing. I could not bear to look. Allessandra would stand a wagon length distant, against a wooden board, while Ubaldo threw the daggers deftly. *Thunk, thunk, thunk.* They would sink into the wood around her, outlining her slim body against the white-painted wood. It was worst when Ubaldo would have her hold pears or apples, or balance them on her head, so that he could send his daggers winging into them. The crowds loved that best of all. But I saw how Allessandra's hands trembled when she came back into the wagon after the shows and how she poured herself a thimbleful of the strong, dark brandy she had hidden away in the wardrobe.

The wardrobe was something I came to know all too well. Allessandra was teaching me her craft, but there was much to learn before I could tell fortunes as she did. In the meantime, she had other work for me. She produced a thin, white chemise with great winglike arms and a pouch of white powder.

"With these, we can turn you into a spirit," she told me with a conspiratorial smile. "It is how I began as well. Easy work. I will do the hard part. You wait in the wardrobe, here." She opened the cabinet and showed me.

"It's a false back," I said, as she slid the wood aside.

"All part of the magic. I call you out during the reading. Everyone has a dead woman somewhere in their family. Mother, sister, wife, daughter."

"How will I know which I am?" I asked.

"Ah, that's the beauty of our trade," she said. "People are so desperate, they will often show you what they want without prompting. If you tell them what they hope to hear, they will believe it. Let's try this on, and you'll see."

Unthinkingly, I unlaced my bodice and pulled off my tattered gown. I had no reason for modesty with Alle, and I was wearing my smalls beneath, in any case. It was only when I'd let the gown fall to the floor of the wagon that I realized the glimmering gold loops of Father's chain of mastery were plainly visible around my waist.

"My, my, what a lovely thing," Allessandra said. "So I was right about your father's mastery, then? He must have great talent to have earned such a prize. That is the gift of a prince or a king."

"The doge of Valenzia," I said. "Please, you won't tell Ubaldo, will you?"

She sniffed, still looking at the gold chain. "To think he has such a treasure under his nose and he doesn't even know it." She smiled, a trifle viciously. When she turned her gaze back on me, her expression lightened. "No, child, have no fear. Your secret is safe. But be very careful. If Ubaldo, or even Coso or Cristo, finds out that you carry such riches, he will take it like that." She snapped her fingers. "Ubaldo always did love taking what others love best." She passed one hand over her belly; the other hand curled at the neck of her glittering robes. For such a tall and impressive woman, she looked suddenly meek and helpless. I started to reach for her shoulder.

Ubaldo shouted from outside. "Hurry it up, woman. I've a crowd waiting for the dagger toss. Do I have to come in there and drag you out?"

Off she went, leaving me to study the tools of my new occupation and to wonder what old sorrow it was that troubled her.

CHAPTER

3

S EVERAL DAYS LATER, I waited in the secret compartment, my hair loose and dusted with the white powder, more of it turning my face pasty. The gauzy gown trailed down over my toes inconveniently, but I would not need to move far. Alle had made me practice opening the secret door dozens of times, blindfolded, one-handed, even backward. "Bad for business if the ghost gets stuck in the wardrobe," she said.

The blue wagon had been fitted with bright fabric to hang over the back, and the movable steps were brought out and set at the rear. Passing up those steps and into the wagon, a patron would find Allessandra the All-Knowing seated before a low table (the trunk, covered in a glimmering black cloth). I had hung up curtains to disguise the mundane elements of our life, turning the interior of the wagon into a dark, magical den swirling with musky incense.

I listened attentively as Alle welcomed her first patron, the first person I would sham. I squashed down that thought mercilessly. Alle had told me the spirit visitations were worth an extra guilder. And she promised to make certain I had a few pennies of that, whatever Ubaldo might say. With Father still recovering, I had to do my part to earn our keep, or we'd be back on the side of the road with no donkey and no hope.

It was a man. I could hear him mumbling, but the words were muffled by the wardrobe. There was a creak as Alle opened the outer doors. "The seeing crystal," she intoned as she took it from the cabinet. It was all part of the act, to give the patron a chance to see that the wardrobe was empty.

"Ahhh," said the man, "and you will be able to tell me what she says?"

Then the doors closed again and it returned to mumbles.

Allessandra's voice, however, was pitched to carry clearly even at a whisper. "It may be that she shall tell you herself, if your love is true and I have strength enough to part the veil."

It went on for a bit, mumble, mumble, then Alle, then more mumbling. My hands grew slick. I rubbed them on the ghost dress. Then, at last: "Spirit, come forth!"

I made one silent prayer to the Saints. It wasn't, as one might expect, asking forgiveness for the deception I was about to engage in. It was that I not get caught. I slipped through the secret panel, then closed it behind me. Flinging open the doors of the wardrobe, I wafted out.

"Maria!" the man cried, rising and holding out both hands toward me. He was tall and lean, with long arms that reached over across the chest, dangerously close. I froze. Alle hadn't said what to do if the patrons tried to touch me. What would they say if they felt soft gauze or, worse, warm flesh, where there should be only ghostly vapor? I backed away.

"Beware," Allessandra warned, "for the touch of the living may force the spirits of the dead to retreat once more. And your wife has come far to speak to you; there must be some important message she has to deliver."

The man clutched his hands together. His brow was wet with perspiration. Mine was as well, for the layers of gauze were surprisingly hot in the stuffy wagon. "Maria, Maria, have you come to tell me of our child? Is she with you, in the Hall of Saints? Oh, tell me it is so."

I was kerflummoxed enough by this to stand silent for a long moment. But Alle had been right. He was telling me exactly what he wanted to hear. I stumbled on, hoping my delay had appeared as but a dramatic pause. "It is so," I intoned.

The man collapsed back into his seat, bowing his head in his hands and rubbing his scraggly hair. He wept. "I knew it, I knew it."

Allessandra took charge once more. "The veil over the spirit world may part for only a short time. Your wife grows weary. She must return to her rest in the Hall of the Saints. You must bid her farewell."

"Maria, I love you! Take care of her until I join you!" he cried, reaching out toward me once more. I evaded him, turning the motion into a slow disapparition. Swaying and waving my arms in their white wings of gauze, I carefully stepped back into the wardrobe. Alle rose and closed the doors, winking at me when her back was turned to the man. I fumbled with the secret panel and got myself hidden away as silently as possible.

Mumble, mumble, I heard the man babbling outside.

Then Alle again. "You are a fortunate man, to have a wife who loves you so dearly that she could endure this visitation."

Then the heavy tread of the man tramping down the steps, leaving the wagon.

My heart was beating quick as a festival drum. The doors creaked open to reveal Alle holding her crystal ball and beaming at me.

"Not so hard, is it? You're a natural." She flashed a bright smile. "Good work. Now, get ready, there's another waiting."

Flushed with victory, I continued playing my part over the next several weeks, portraying dozens of dead women from village to village. I perfected a wide variety of theatrical groans, moans, and a whispery, sepulchral voice. Meanwhile, Father steadily improved, and by the time three Saints' Days came and went, he was fully recovered.

By then Alle had already taught me much, and truth be told, I was enjoying it. I continued to play my part as the spirit in the wardrobe, but I was also learning to tell fortunes myself. She taught me the clues to look for, the hints that could tell her where a person was from, what they did, whom they loved, more than I ever would have thought possible to learn from so little. The color of the mud on their boots. The different types of calluses that revealed wheelwright, cooper, shoemaker, smith, farmer. The lines of laughter and sorrow that marked a face, and the scars of wounds and illness.

"You have a talent for it," she told me one day. "I could tell, when you saw how I read your own past. And of course, the best fortune-teller must always know what is magic and what is not, and never begin to think that she is more than she truly is. You do not believe in magic, so that is not a danger you need fear. Now, what can you tell from this piece of cloth?"

And so it continued. I accumulated a store of information on a variety of obscure topics. I knew all the weaves of the great fabric mills throughout the land. I knew the different dyes, and which patterns were popular in which cities. I learned to identify the subtle variations in dialect, how folk from the southern principalities would lisp their S's, and folk from Sirenza, where the streets were of water, gave each vowel sound a sharp inflection.

Father returned to work, but we remained with Ubaldo and his company. It was something like sleeping with lions, but we had no choice. He would not give us back Franca, and without her we had no wagon, and with no wagon Father could not work. Besides, we were eating better than we had in over a year. The hard part was convincing Ubaldo to allow us to stay.

WE HAD HALTED in the open market green at the center of the village. The blue wagon was set up as usual for Allessandra the All-Knowing. Our own was parked nearby, and I rounded up a crowd with my cries of "Shoes! Boots! Fancy footgear for a fair price!" As I mingled, I listened to the villagers and looked for calluses, stains, unsteady walks, practicing what Alle was teaching me. A woman in a red bonnet complained shrilly that her swain cared more for his coracle and fish than he did for her, and contemplated pitching him over for the baker. A man spare and pale as a winter birch said nothing, but tapped the fingers of his left hand together incessantly. I sidled

35

closer and saw the callus on his right middle finger. A clerk, mindful still of his calculations and ledgers, even at market. Nearby, two young lads chattered excitedly about how a rogue mercenary captain had taken over Sirenza and imprisoned its king, and whether they might make good money if they joined one of the roving mercenary bands themselves.

Father made the first pair of shoes for a doughty farmwife in a hamlet outside Roltino. They were sunset orange with blue fringes, but at least (I saw with a sigh of relief) they fit. The woman went off shaking her head, peering down past her own generous girth and flinching each time she caught sight of her feet. Several other villagers who had already paid their deposits and been measured looked uneasily at one another.

Ubaldo had been glowering over the scene from a short distance, tossing his ever-present dagger with increasing vigor. He grabbed my elbow as I went by. "What's the meaning of this? Those shoes are horrible! What sort of fool is your father to make such ugly things?"

"My father is the best shoemaker in Valenzia."

"Hah. Well, he's not in Valenzia now, and I'd say he's the worst shoemaker in all the lands. They'll run us out of town. And it'll be your fault." He glared at me. "I'll leave you right back where I found you, no doubt of that, girl! And worse yet if you cost me coin."

I had to do something. I was afraid Ubaldo was right about the villagers. They were muttering angrily as Father cut a length of violently green suede. But my work with Alle and the memory of the shoes I had sold back in Valenzia gave me an idea.

"Magic," I said. Without looking at Ubaldo, I hurried over to the wagon, shouting all the way. "Magic boots! Get them here! Crafted with the magic of the fairies themselves, they will bring good luck and happiness to the one who wears them!" Father started, and blinked at me from under his bushy brows. He opened his mouth, but I shook my head and continued on brazenly. "Magic boots, once-in-a-lifetime chance! Get them here!"

The woman in the red bonnet, the one I'd eavesdropped on earlier, snorted at me. "Magic, hah. The only magic they have is that they'll never be stolen. Who would want such ugly things?"

I thought quickly, running through what I had overheard earlier. "Ah, but with such shoes as these, you will surely catch the eye of that certain someone. Sailors are known to favor fancy footwear, you know. These shoes are meant for walking under the crossed boughs at a great cathedral. Surely you would be willing to pay a few guilders to have that happiness."

Her face grew white, and she opened and closed her mouth. "How did you . . . ? They will, truly?" She gave my father a considering look. I took her arm and gently led her to Father. "Just two guilders, but what is coin, compared to your future happiness?"

Two guilders barely covered the materials, but it was better than nothing. I babbled on for a bit. When I left her, the red-capped woman was misty with dreams of a cathedral wedding and showers of blossoms. The disgruntled edge to the gossip of the crowd had been replaced by a buzz of excitement. Father was so busy I started taking down orders myself.

"Nata," he whispered aside to me, during a lull, "whatever made you say that? You know I've lost the magic. They're shoes, nothing more."

"Shush, Papa, please. Just trust me."

The marks I made taking down measurements were dark and sharp with my frustration. Why couldn't he simply believe they were magic? He believed other things that weren't true. I'd been trying so hard to make things work with Alle and Ubaldo, to keep us fed and safe. I'd already lost one comfortable life. I didn't want to lose the hope of another. But thankfully Father heeded my warning and did not speak of it again.

When I had collected the last of the coins, I breathed a great sigh of relief. The pouch was pleasantly heavy in my hand, and would be more so when the patrons returned to collect their finished shoes and pay their balances. I wondered if it would be enough to buy back Franca. The thought that Ubaldo still possessed her irked me to no end. I did not care for being dependent on him, much as I had grown to like Alle.

There was enough, I decided, that I could spare a guilder for some fresh nut cakes, sweet and dripping with spiced honey. I could smell them from the bakery across the market grounds. Father loved sweets, and we hadn't had any in ever so long.

Something silvery flashed through the air a hand span from my nose. A meaty, gold-ringed fist caught the knife. "You did well enough out there," Ubaldo said, tossing the dagger dangerously close to my face once again. "But remember my warning, girl. Alle may like you, but to me you're just a piece of baggage, you and your father both. You weigh us down, you get left at the side of the road."

"You call this weighing you down?" I said, holding up the pouch of coin. "It's at least as much as you made with your last performance."

Before I could protest, Ubaldo had tweaked the pouch from my hand. "And a good start toward repaying your debt."

"What?" I said, fury driving my voice high and shrill. "That's ours, rightfully earned!"

"You'd have earned nothing back at the side of the North Road, eaten by wolves or murdered by bandits. Remember that it was I who took pity on you then."

"You did nothing—"

He moved faster than I could see, clouting me across the chin with the heavy bag of coins. I staggered back, eyes smarting. I might have lunged at him then and there, but he waggled the silver blade. "Off with you, girl, you've work to do. Cristo needs someone to scrape the carrots. Quick now, if you want any supper."

He swaggered away, whistling a merry tune. I sniffed, trying to clear the sob from my throat. My lip was bleeding slightly. The metallic taste soured the scent of the nut cakes, but that was just as well. There would be none tonight, nor any night to come. Not until I could find a way to outsmart Ubaldo.

I SCRAPED AND CHOPPED carrots with great vehemence that night, imagining that it was Ubaldo under my knife. I wanted to run away, back to Valenzia, back to the life I had known, where I always had a spare coin for one of Zia Rosa's nut cakes. Where my mother would have slipped her arm around my shoulders and washed my cut lip and made me laugh with tales of the puffed-up lords and ladies who'd come to order footwear that day. But running away wouldn't bring Mother back. And it would mean leaving the wagon and all our supplies behind, for I didn't have a hope of stealing Franca away under Ubaldo's watchful eye.

When I brought Father his bowl of soup, I ducked my

head to cast my swollen lip in shadow. He wouldn't have noticed it even if it was midday, though. He was thoroughly engaged in his work. I had hoped that with the encouragement of so many patrons, not to mention my little deception about the magical nature of the shoes, he might have recovered his lost artistry. Maybe then we could risk leaving behind the wagon and returning to Valenzia on the promise of future wealth. Or simply refuse to travel onward with Ubaldo when we reached the next large city. But no, these shoes were as hideous as the last.

Despair pulled at me, tightening my throat. I breathed the steam rising from the soup. I had to be calm. Father needed me to be strong, like Mother.

"You see, Papa, you haven't lost your magic," I said with false cheer, setting the bowl down beside his knee. He sat cross-legged against the wagon wheel, hunched over the purple and green leather he was stitching together with a length of waxed orange floss.

Father leaned back, squinting at the shoes through his thick spectacles. They had slipped down to the very tip of his nose. He sighed and shook his head. "No, Nata, the magic was never mine. It was in the tools, and now it's gone. The fairies have forgotten me. Look at those."

I followed his gesture to the array of tools on the cloth beside him. My heart fell. They were crusted with bits of leather dust, paint, wax, and even rust now.

"Papa, why don't you just clean them yourself? Or let me do it. You're the Master Shoemaker of Valenzia, don't you remember? The doge gave you the gold chain. Surely that means something. And look at how many people wanted to buy your shoes today!"

"Because you said they were magic."

"They are as much magic as they ever were. You just have to make them as you used to. With proper colors, and so that they match each other."

"Hmm? You don't like the colors? What's wrong with them?"

I gave up. "Eat your soup, Papa—it's getting cold. We pay dearly enough to travel with Ubaldo. Don't waste the few crumbs he gives us." Father was blind if he couldn't see what was wrong with his shoes. And he hadn't even asked me about my lip.

Allessandra, on the other hand, watched me intently when I returned to the campfire and dipped up my own bowl of noodles. Ubaldo had procured a large skin of wine (probably with the coins he'd stolen from me) and was sharing it with Coso and Cristo. The three of them had become increasingly merry as the skin grew more and more limp. But when I trod on Ubaldo's foot accidentally, that jollity vanished like a mist in morning. "Stupid girl!" he roared. "Watch your step!" He raised one fist to swipe at me. I stood there stupidly, not having learned yet to be on guard against such sudden violence. But two things prevented that blow from falling. The drink had already slowed Ubaldo's wits, making the motion slow and clumsy. And Allessandra pulled me back.

Ubaldo roared and raised his fist again as Coso and Cristo hooted with laughter. Allessandra had me behind her by then. "Now, my dear, would you like a nut cake? The local baker claims to make the best in all the lands, and you know how you love them." She held out the round brown sweet to Ubaldo, smiling more serenely than I could have, with that great gilded fist hovering so close.

"And more wine?" she continued, taking up the wineskin in her other hand. "You've worked so hard today, you deserve to enjoy yourself. Never mind the girl, she's not worth your trouble."

"Bah!" Ubaldo snatched the cake and wineskin from her hands, still glowering. "Just keep her out of my way. Stupid, clumsy brat." He sat back and munched on the cake.

Allessandra squeezed my hand warningly.

"Ah, give us some," Coso said. "I love a good nut cake."

"You'll buy your own," said Ubaldo. "I'm the leader of this company. All of you remember that."

"Pass the wine, then, at least," said Cristo.

Ubaldo tossed back the last bite of the cake, then squirted a copious amount of wine into his mouth.

Dribbles of red ran through his curling beard and down his front. "Ah!" He smacked his lips and threw the nearly empty skin to Cristo. "There you go, boys. I'm done. The rest is yours."

Coso and Cristo fell to bickering over the dregs, and eventually the three men departed altogether, in search of an alehouse. Allessandra kept tight hold of my wrist all this time.

She watched the men until they disappeared in the gloom of evening across the greensward. Then she turned dark, troubled eyes on me at last. She reached out and brushed a finger over my tender lip, a crease marring the lovely white skin between her brows. "Ubaldo?"

"He stole them!" My words burst out like a summer storm, carrying with them all the rage and frustration that had been thundering inside since Ubaldo struck me. "He took all the coins Father earned. He stole them, just as he stole Franca!" I brushed a hand across my eyes, feeling the pricking of tears.

"Shush," she warned. "If you haven't learned by now not to accuse him of such things, you're not as clever as I thought. Now, let me find a poultice for that lip, or it will be a pretty sight tomorrow. It's already bruising a bit." She looked past me to the wagon, where Father was still hard at work.

"He won't notice, even if it does bruise," I said bitterly. I wiped my eyes again.

Her gaze flicked back to me. She slipped her arm around my shoulders. "How long has it been since you lost your mother?"

"Two years, come the Feast of Saint Lucia." That was when I'd gotten the dress with the red ribbons. I remembered Mother stitching them on carefully. How excited I had been, wheedling for a chance to wear it early, getting underfoot and hanging about at her elbow until she'd sent me away so that she might finish the work before the celebration.

"It must be hard. You're no more than a girl. But you've taken good care of your father."

I shrugged. "He loves me very much, I know that. But he doesn't take heed of things. Not like a normal father might. I've had to manage our money, our food, everything." My brittle control cracked. Everything had gone so horribly wrong. I couldn't do this. I wasn't supposed to do this. How could the Saints have taken my mother away? Didn't they know how much we—I— needed her?

The words came tumbling out, the whole story of our fall from wealth and esteem to poverty and disgrace. Allessandra listened. With my eyes clogged by tears, I could almost imagine it was my mother there, quiet and serene and wise. Her arm steadied my trembling shoulders. Cool fingers brushed my hand, pressing a handkerchief into my palm.

When I had finished, I sat staring into the fire. My cheeks were hot from the flames, or shame, or anger, I couldn't tell which. After some time had passed, Allessandra spoke.

"The world is a hard place. You've seen the folk who come to me, seeking answers, seeking sense. Wanting to know that some bright future is before them."

"And it isn't," I said bleakly. "That's just a lie we make up, to get their coin to fill our own bellies. Or Ubaldo's, rather."

"Whether or not there is magic, or fairies, or trolls, or dragons in the world, there is love. You've done much already out of love for your father. You will go far with that love, and you will make a better life for yourself."

"You see it, with your All-Knowing eyes?" I said sarcastically.

"I know it, and it is true. But you must be wary. Do not stay with Ubaldo any longer than you need. He is an evil man."

"You're here," I pointed out.

"Only as long as I must be."

"Alle," I said, emboldened by the confessional tone of our talk, "how did you come to this life? Were you born to it?" I had often wondered. Allessandra was still a young woman, perhaps a dozen years older than myself.

Her laugh was lovely as always, but it held a bitter edge, like sour-orange jam. "I was born in the East, in a beautiful city with pigeons in the plaza who would peck the bread crusts in my hand. I had a father too, back then."

"What happened?"

"A story not unlike your own. Except that when we fell into poverty, my father sold me to a traveling troupe of entertainers."

My mouth gaped as I imagined such a thing. "That's horrible! How could he?"

She shook her head. "I don't even know that much, for he never said good-bye. I don't know who I hate more, my father for abandoning me, or Ubaldo for . . ."

She trailed off. I said nothing but thanked the Saints that at least I knew Papa loved me, for all his other faults.

"But that's in the past. I've learned much since then, and I've a few tricks up my sleeve." She reached into the voluminous folds of her robe and extricated a wrinkled dried leaf of a strange silvery color. She held it out, grinning. "Dreamwell. A leaf of that, and even a man of Ubaldo's size will be asleep within the hour. He'll be passed out across the bar at the alehouse by now."

"How—"

"Slipped into the center of the nut cake. My special spice. He never noticed it, with the honey and cinnamon to cover the taste. But I can't use it every day. It would kill him."

"And that would be a bad thing?"

She smiled. "Perhaps not for the world. But I do not want that stain on my soul. For now, I know enough to get by with my wits and a bit of dreamwell here and there. You must do the same. If I could—" Whatever she had been going to say, apparently she thought better of it. "You must learn to outsmart him," she said. "Learn to slip a few coins into a secret pocket. I'll show you how to sew one into your gown. You keep those coins, for you and your father. When you have enough, you buy a donkey and you get away from Ubaldo. Do you understand?"

I nodded.

THE DAYS PASSED QUICKLY. I continued to hate Ubaldo and to despise Coso and Cristo for their sycophantic admiration of him. But I enjoyed my work, and even better was the clink of the coins in my secret purse. Every pair of shoes Father made fed that purse a penny, as did every one of my ghostly manifestations. More than that, and Ubaldo would have noticed. But the dribs and drabs I could ferret away. I hid the purse among the leather, rolled up in a rich brown hide that Father never used.

I earned a few more bruises from Ubaldo before I grew quick enough to evade them, and to recognize his foulest moods and stay clear during them. I wondered how many Allessandra had suffered when she first joined the troupe. Or suffered yet. More than once, I caught her swabbing white grease over her neck to cover a suspicious red-purple mark. At least I could avoid Ubaldo at night, cuddled in my blanket under the wagon, near Father. But Allessandra had to endure his foul moods and temper even then, and perhaps far worse than I could imagine.

Nevertheless, she was always perfectly serene when we went about our work. She blithely took any fool with guilders and fed him her beautiful lies. I did not mind it so much when it was fat merchants, but I did have a few sleepless nights after we'd told a half-starved young fellow that he would become a great minstrel and turn his songs into gold.

"Songs into gold?" I said, after that one. "I told you he had a lute player's calluses, not that he was an alchemist!"

"He just needed a bit of encouragement," Allessandra said, unruffled. "You heard him speak. Can you tell me you don't think that voice will earn him gold? That guilder he paid was the best coin he ever spent."

"It looked as if he'd have done better to spend it on a good meal, not our lies."

"Now then, child, have some respect for our craft. A meal will feed him for a day, but the hope we gave him, that will last for years."

And so it went. Before I knew it, my Saint's Day had

come and gone, and I was a year older. Surreptitiously, I began to price donkeys and to estimate how far we could get if we fled while the men were off in an alehouse. We could leave now, if only I sold the doge's chain. But I knew I could get barely a fraction of its worth, ragtag as I was. Or, worse, such a treasure as that might mark me a thief in some eyes.

I couldn't do it. That chain was the greatest acknowledgment Father had ever received. Now it was all he had left. If I sold the chain to be melted down, divided up, it would be as if that skill had been no more real than Father's fairies. And it had been real!

It could still return too. We could go back to Valenzia, Father triumphantly attired in the finest silks, wearing a fabulous pair of his own boots, with this gold necklace heavy upon his breast. Our patrons would return, bearing gifts and clamoring for Father to create new boots, shoes, and slippers. Nothing could make me abandon that dream, not even Ubaldo.

He was in a particularly black mood today. His morning show had been heckled by a crowd of young noblemen, and when he'd confronted them, they had set their men on him. It was rare to see Ubaldo cut or even bruised. Now he was a mess of darkening flesh, and one eye had swollen shut, giving him an even fiercer appearance than normal. Bad as they looked, these injuries were only a pale reflection of the fury inside. I had already suffered a particularly nasty wallop after I put thyme in the soup rather than oregano. Even Coso and Cristo had retreated to the local alehouse.

I bundled Father up into the wagon to work, making him promise to stay out of Ubaldo's way. Allessandra tried to keep her distance too, but Ubaldo demanded that she wait on him as he lounged by the campfire, tossing knives at a nearby sapling that was quickly turning to splinters. Ubaldo had already finished a skin of wine. Now he was rapidly working his way through another, becoming more ill-tempered as he went. Allessandra sent me off to fetch nut cakes, hoping they would divert him from the wine, at least for a time. "A bit of my secret spice, then he'll be fast asleep, and we'll have some peace and no broken bones," she'd said.

As I returned with my basket of sweets and heard the angry bellows, my feet slowed of their own accord. Even nut cakes could not soothe that temper. Why risk going any nearer? I might as well confront a bear in its den. Then I heard Allessandra's cry.

When I ran out of the shadows into the dancing light of the campfire, I saw her crumpled on the earth. Ubaldo stood over her, calling her terrible names I didn't even know the meaning of—and I had heard a fair bit by then. Something glittered in the firelight. He held a dagger. By the Saints, no, he was going to kill her! I hurtled into him, trying to push him away from her. This was as effective as a bird throwing itself into the side of a bear, but it did startle him enough that he dropped the dagger. With another roar, he brought his great fist sweeping down at me. The nut cakes flew in every direction. I fell back beside Allessandra. She moaned weakly. Ubaldo had clipped my chin with the blow. I looked up, dazed, expecting to see him looming over me. But he wasn't there.

Blearily I looked around. Ubaldo had staggered a few steps away and was staring at something on the ground. He stooped. I grew cold. It was the dagger, and he was going to kill us both.

But what he picked up from the grass glimmered gold, not silver.

"That's mine!" I croaked, some part of my brain still fighting, still thinking I could beat him with pure energy and rage.

"So you've been holding out on me, have you?" His voice was dangerously quiet. "I thought as much. I could tell you were a little rat. This is a fine thing, must have come from a king."

"A doge," I corrected him. "It belongs to my father. He is the Master Shoemaker of Valenzia."

"Well, we can all see he's that no longer," Ubaldo said. "So as that's the way of things, I'll keep this."

"No!" I started to push myself up, ignoring the dizziness, but a nearby moan gave me pause. "Saints' shadows!" I hissed, seeing Allessandra's bloodied face. She looked like a demon from the stained-glass depictions of the seven Hells I'd seen in the cathedral.

As Ubaldo walked past, he spat on the grass near Allessandra. "And you. You knew about this; I can see it in your eyes. Just be glad I didn't break your legs this time."

Ubaldo tramped off, leaving Allessandra and me by the campfire. I mopped the blood from her face as best I could. It streamed from her nose. I hoped it looked worse than it was. She smiled weakly up at me, covering my bloody hand with her own. "I'm sorry about the chain. Truly."

"At least it put him in a good mood," I said, gently pulling free of her grip. "He's cheerful as a jester now."

"If he weren't, I would probably be dead." Allessandra pushed herself up, wincing.

"Here," I said, cradling her shoulders. "Lean on me."

"But you've lost your chain."

"Don't worry. I'll be getting it back. I swear by Saint Fortunata on that. And Saint Ubaldo too, for that matter." I grimaced, dabbing at the blood that would not stop flowing from her battered nose. I feared Ubaldo had broken it.

Allessandra drew away and looked at me seriously. "Fortunata, child, thank you for trying to help me. He would have killed me. You remember what I told you, about getting away from him. Promise me you will do that."

"You're getting blood on your robes," I said. "Here, press that to your nose."

She took the handkerchief, but her eyes remained fast on mine. "Promise me."

"I promise," I said. Once I get Father's chain back, I added silently.

She sank back down then and let me finish washing the blood from her face. I collected the fallen nut cakes and gave her one, but she only nibbled at it. She kept one hand tightly clenched on a lump under her skirt: her own secret hidden pouch.

I left her there, to take Father one of the nut cakes. "What was the shouting?" he asked.

"Just Ubaldo. As usual."

"That man, he's a bad one," he said, taking off his spectacles and wiping them. He squinted at me. "Are you all right, Nata?"

"Yes, Papa," I said. But when he reached out to hug me, I crumpled against him. I clung there as he stroked my hair and hummed an old song Mother had sung years ago, until at last my belly unclenched and I fell asleep.

CHAPTER

4

U BALDO'S BELLOWS woke me before dawn. "That
harridan!" he thundered. "That ungrateful witch!
Where is she?"

Allessandra was gone. We searched the blue wagon,
we searched every shop in town. All the while, Ubaldo
continued to boil like an untended pot, frothing and
fuming. He lashed out at anyone who got near enough. I
took Father with me to walk along the bridle path that
looped around to the west, through a wooded area
twisted with bramble. Father had work to do, but better
he not be left alone with Ubaldo in this state.

We met a single traveler, a cleric on donkey-back, on
his way to the great cathedral of Sirenza. He had seen no
one of Allessandra's description.

"I hope Mistress Allessandra is all right," Father said, as the cleric trundled on ahead of us.

I didn't know what to think. Had she left? Fear shriveled my nerves, chased fast by anger. I tried to quash them. Allessandra wouldn't have abandoned me here with Ubaldo. "Maybe she went on a walk, to get away from Ubaldo for a little while."

"He's a bad one," Father said, as he had last night. "Do you suppose, Nata, that we should leave?"

Such initiative from my father boggled me for a moment, but I collected my wits and shook my head. "We will leave, Papa, but not yet. We need a donkey to pull our wagon. And Ubaldo has—" I decided not to mention the gold chain. Father hadn't paid it much heed before this; he'd probably forgotten it even existed. But if I told him Ubaldo had it and that was why we were staying, who knew what Father might do. "Ubaldo has never treated you poorly, has he, Papa?"

Father shook his head. He was still frowning at me. "But, Nata, you—"

"I'll be quite all right, Papa, just you see." I took his hand and squeezed it. Father smiled his gentle smile, and my heart warmed despite my fears.

"Nata, look there," he said, squinting past me.

There was a tiny scrap of bright blue fabric caught in the thorns of a bramble bush at the side of the narrow track. I pulled it loose and held it in a shaft of sunlight. It glittered where a small sequin caught the light. It was Allessandra's, I had no doubt.

"I hope she gets far away from here," Father said, his mellow voice more firm than usual.

The blows I'd suffered at Ubaldo's hand were nothing to the pain I felt then. Allessandra had abandoned me. I steadied myself against the bole of a nearby tree. I was alone. Again. My future loomed darker and bleaker than ever before, and I had no Alle there to pat my shoulder and teach me how to survive. When I drew my breath, it caught in my clogged throat. Father blinked at me. "Nata?"

I pushed myself away from the tree. Saints, help me, I couldn't let Father see how terrified I was. I should have known it was up to me, only me, to keep us together and safe. Allessandra had been kind, very kind, during our time together. But in the end, she had looked out for herself. I would have to do the same.

In any case, I had already determined to stay and get my father's gold chain back from that pig Ubaldo. Had Allessandra known that? Was that why she hadn't asked me to come? I remembered her making me promise to leave. She must have been planning her own escape even then. I clutched the bit of sparkling cloth more tightly.

I heard voices approaching behind us on the track, from the direction of town. I could tell without looking that one of them was Ubaldo. "She couldn't have gotten that far, curse it, weak bit of a thing that she is. How dare she think she can run off on me!"

They rounded the curve of the track, just as I tucked the scrap of blue cloth away in my pouch. I might be angry with Allessandra for leaving us, but I would not betray her to Ubaldo.

"She hasn't come this way," I called out as soon as he saw us. Better to deliver the bad news from a distance.

Ubaldo roared, but fortunately for me Cristo was the closest at hand. Ubaldo collared the fellow, nearly lifting him up off the ground. "You, this is your fault! You slug, you worm, you lazy piece of dung. You should have caught her before she set foot outside the camp!"

Cristo choked something out that sounded like a protest. His face turned faintly purple. Ubaldo tossed the man aside—into a stand of brambles, judging by Cristo's yelps—and turned on Father and me.

"You!" he said, his dark eyes bulging under his red bald head, fierce teeth gleaming white in the darkness of his beard. "You helped her. The two of you were always whispering together behind my back!"

"No, sir, I had nothing to do with it," I said. "Why should I want her to leave? Now I have no work. I can't play the ghost if there's no medium."

Ubaldo fell silent, but those great black eyes were burning into me. "No medium, eh?" he said at last. "No more Allessandra the All-Knowing?" He shook his head.

"Not if all the Saints so willed it. The fortune-telling brings in half our coin. We will have fortunes to sell, by the seven Hells. You will do it." He jabbed one gold-ringed finger at me.

"I will?"

"She's trained you up well enough, or so she told me. It best be true, else I'll think all this soup and porridge I've been so generous as to share has been going to waste. Allessandra taught you her craft. Now you'll put it to use."

"Me, tell the fortunes? But—"

Ubaldo flexed his fingers. I fell silent.

"Nata, dear Nata, do you truly have the gift?" Father exclaimed. "Your mother always said you had a touch of magic, you know."

Ubaldo chuckled. "Yes, shoemaker, your daughter will have magic aplenty, if she knows what's good for both of you. Now get back there, girl. You'll be performing this very noon. You too, old man, back to work!"

I clamped my mouth shut and tugged Father with me, past Ubaldo. Father was still chattering excitedly. "Such tales you told as a wee thing. And of course Saint Fortunata is the patron of sages and prophets. Ah, what joy it brings me to know that even if my magic is gone, you have found some of your own!"

I tried to shush him. "It's no magic—it's just what Allessandra taught me. Trickery, that's all." But he kept bubbling up like a forest spring. I had no time to argue further; I had to marshal my resources for what was to come. Despite myself, my head filled with images of glory, of the lines of petitioners come seeking the wisdom of Fortunata the All-Knowing. I saw myself standing before doges, queens, great lords and ladies, all begging me to reveal that greatest of mysteries, the truth they already knew.

Then I shivered, the bright dream crumpling under my fears. If I failed, Father and I might end up on the side of the road with nothing but our ragged clothes and broken dreams. Could I really do this? What if they laughed or, worse, discovered I was a fraud? Allessandra had indeed taught me much, but was it enough for me to take her place?

I certainly could not match her striking appearance. For one thing, I lacked a proper costume. Allessandra had taken most of her things, leaving only a ragged red-and-black robe that had lost most of its sequins. At least the headdress remained: a peaked hat crowned by a silver moon and stars, trailing a long black scarf that could be wrapped around my hair to disguise the mouse-brown color. It had an unfortunate tendency to slide sideways off my head, but by dint of several pins I managed to fix it in place. That left only my face, which looked childish and round in the midst of the severe black and red and silver of the costume. At least Allessandra had not taken her paints.

With my eyes ringed in kohl, skin paled with white powder, and lips reddened by paint, I looked like something inhuman. It would have to do. At least it was better than looking like the scared girl that I felt inside.

The first patron was an easy one, thank the Saints. A girl, wanting to know whether she should agree to her parents' wishes and give herself at the cathedral to become a chaste cleric of the Saints. I could tell at once that she had some other wish.

"There is another path," I said, pausing for her to fill in the details.

"Oh, please, tell me, is there a lad? A lad with sandy hair and blue eyes like cornflowers?"

"Yes, he stands beckoning to you, calling you. But you do not come, there is some obstacle. . . ." I knew there must be, else this girl would be wedded already. Clearly she loved the boy with the cornflower-blue eyes.

"Oh, it's all Mama's fault," the girl complained. "Why can't she see that a shepherd is good enough for me? I will be happy. I don't need a rich house and a servant as she does. Better a cold house with my love than a cold heart in the richest cathedral."

As usual, the girl had told her own fortune well enough—she just could not see it. But now it was for me to cast it back to her, with the proper trappings, so that she would believe the message of her own heart.

"I see a lad, a lad with blue eyes like cornflowers. He

comes to your house, he kneels before your mother and asks for her blessing. I see you stepping forth from your house, arm in arm with the lad. You stand together under the crossed boughs, before the cleric in her white robes. And more, I see a house, a large flock of sheep and children running with the lambs, and a cozy fire burning in the hearth. You will grow old there together, and though the winds may whistle and bring chill, you have merriment and love in your hearts to warm you."

The girl departed the wagon with a string of thanks, nearly stumbling over her own feet in her haste. "Oh, thank you, thank you! We'll go to my mother at once. And if she won't give her blessing, well then we'll go to the cleric ourselves."

I watched her go, feeling a brief twinge of guilt. Perhaps it was wrong to direct her toward a life that would certainly be harsher than the security of a cleric's lot. But it was the path the girl herself wanted, and if nothing else, Allessandra had taught me that people will not accept a fortune they do not really want to come to pass. I sent up a short prayer to the Saints that they would watch over the girl and her shepherd. Maybe they would have the warm hearth and the children and the love I had foretold.

OVER TIME, I learned to clamp down on the twinges of guilt, push them back into the corners of my mind. A conscience was not particularly useful in my new trade. Father and I needed every penny I could squeeze out of this work, if we were to purchase a donkey and escape from Ubaldo. I managed to set aside a coin or two from every fee, and the occasional extra gratuity for a particularly well-received fortune. Slowly, slowly, my pouch grew heavier.

We traveled east, toward Sirenza. It was about two months after I had taken over as prophetess that we arrived at the village of Baltriporto, across the river from the city itself. We halted the wagons in a cobbled square bordered on three sides by shops. On the fourth side, a wide thoroughfare sloped down to the banks of the river Balta. It was a bustling place, full of sailors and merchants and travelers. Boats of all kinds crowded the waters, from huge barges to tiny coracles. I could see Sirenza out upon the water. The gilded dome of the great cathedral rose higher than any other building, its single spire pricking the clear blue sky. The city sat on a triangle of land in the mouth of the Balta, where it ran out into the wider waters of the sea, but canals and waterways cut through the city, leaving only fragments of dry land upon which stood those distant glittering edifices.

I had my reservations about approaching this close. The rumors said that Sirenza had fallen under the control of a ruthless mercenary captain who had taken the city from its rightful king. That sort of thing was common enough. The princes and doges might have gold aplenty, but it was the captains who had the strength of arms. It was an easy step from being hired to defend a city to taking it for oneself.

These rumors were particularly disturbing, however. The man who had taken Sirenza was called the Bloody Captain, for reasons I could only suppose. He had slain the leading members of any family in Sirenza that stood against him. The whole of the king's line had been murdered, leaving no rightful heir to challenge him. Trade and business continued to flow into and out of Sirenza, but the captain's army assessed steep taxes on merchandise. I caught some of this from the rumblings of the merchants as they passed toward the riverbank. But no one spoke above a grumble or whisper.

I knew why. I saw the string of six bodies hung over the wall when we entered Baltriporto, under placards naming them insurgents. Inwardly I cursed Ubaldo for bringing us into such a place.

"Ah," Ubaldo said, rubbing his palms together as he grinned over the crowds, "a fine place. If we do well, we might even pay fare on a boat and try the city itself."

Saints, I hoped not! It was bad enough to be here in Baltriporto. I saw armed men everywhere, lounging against storefronts, hunched over dice, flirting with blushing girls, watching the bustle of the market with distant, cold eyes. I watched as one soldier seized the mugs from the hands of two old men at the alehouse, then gulped down both drinks himself. He tossed the mugs aside carelessly. They cracked against the cobbled street.

I averted my gaze as the soldier glanced toward me. He leered but, thankfully, continued on into the alehouse. Saints keep me, I didn't know if I could lie to such men. Men with swords, men who spilled blood for a living and, from the look of it, enjoyed their work. My throat tightened; my lips already felt too dry and stiff to form words.

I tried to steady my nerves by studying the other armed men, picking out the scars and stains and fabric weaves that could help me navigate these treacherous waters. I needed to do my job now; fear would only get in the way. Coso and Cristo had begun their performance, spinning three bottles through the air between them, along with two apples and a loaf of stale bread. The circle of onlookers grew. Ubaldo glowered at me. Quickly, I ducked into the blue wagon and threw on my fortune-telling costume.

I had already given a handful of fortunes and was in the midst of predicting a bright future for a proud father-to-be when I heard the disturbance outside. Well, it wasn't exactly a disturbance. Rather, it was a sudden hush that raised prickles on the nape of my neck. The father-to-be chattered on blithely, telling me how strong the baby was, how it moved and kicked in his wife's belly, and how that must be a sign that the child would have a great future. Sharp footfalls on the steps brought me to my feet, just as a figure threw open the curtains at the back of the wagon.

I felt as if I were falling into a cold, dank well. I knew that swaggering walk, though it had been more than a year since I had last seen it. Captain Niccolo of Valenzia. He stood for a moment framed in the brightness of the doorway, arms crossed, observing us. I suspected he was waiting for his eyes to adjust to the gloom of the wagon interior. When the father-to-be saw who had entered the wagon, he shrank back toward the small table on which sat my crystal gazing ball. I could see his lips forming words, but he gave only a weak whimper.

"You," the captain ordered. "Leave. Now."

The father-to-be stumbled out of the wagon, helped on his way by a brusque shove. Niccolo pulled out the stool. He tossed back his rich velvet cape with a flourish that served both to draw attention to that fine garment and to disentangle it from his long sword as he sat. "Now, then, I wish to have my fortune told," he began. As his gaze turned fully upon me, he paused, eyes narrowing. "Well, well," he said at last. "Dear little Fortunata, all grown up and lying for a living, are you? And to think you chided me as a thief and ne'er-do-well. So, we meet once more, by the grace of the Saints."

"The Saints have nothing to do with it, if my prayers counted for anything," I snapped.

"Tsk, tsk. You'd better watch your tongue in this strange land. You're no longer in Valenzia, you know."

"Nor are you," I said. "What are you doing here?"

"It's I who came to ask the questions. I'll pay, no fear." He flipped a single coin onto the table. It spun on its end once, then fell with a loud clink to glimmer gold upon the dark wood.

I glared at the gold coin. "I have no fortune for the likes of you."

"Come, now, don't tell me you couldn't use that coin. Put some meat on those scrawny bones you've got hidden under that hideous costume. How long has it been since you had something pretty to wear, or a bath, or even a decent meal?"

"I don't want your charity. And since you think my fortunes are lies anyway, there's no point to my reading yours."

"Ah, but you're wrong there. I have a great interest in hearing you prophesy for me. Tell me my fortune. Tell me what you see, and if you are correct, you may keep that coin."

I opened my mouth to protest, but he moved so quickly the words turned into a breathless gasp. He had the sword out and the tip resting gently against the skin of my throat. "But if you will not, or if the fortune is false, then I will tell you your own future. And it will be short and painful."

I leaned back, but the tip of his sword followed after me. All right, then. I would do it. I was in a fey mood by then, with a sword at my neck and this man I hated standing before me. I looked Niccolo up and down, ignoring his arrogant smile. He was, if possible, dressed even more richly and ostentatiously than he had been in Valenzia. His doublet was black velvet, and the under-shirt beneath was of red silk. They fitted him better than the garments he'd worn in Valenzia. His dark hair hung curling to his shoulders as before, but he now sported a short beard and mustache, which only partially con-cealed a new scar, perhaps but three months old, that slashed across his right cheek. I flicked my gaze over the rogue, finding the clues Allessandra had taught me to spy. I looked last at his hands. They were gloved. Was it my imagination, or had he flinched, just slightly, under my gaze? I remembered the rumors I had heard a year ago. Yes, I could read his past and present well enough.

"You are a man of great power and high ambition," I said, "but cruel and merciless. You grew tired of being simply a hired sword for greater men and tried to step higher. But in Valenzia you failed, and you bear the mark of this failure there. Beneath that glove lies the mark of your true nature, the murderer."

Niccolo's eyes narrowed; for a brief moment, his

nonchalance parted and I could see the cold brutality beneath. Then he shrugged, smirking, and nodded for me to continue.

"You turned your attention to a different city. Sirenza, the waterborne city. You came as Captain Niccolo, but you earned a different name. The Bloody Captain slew all opposition and took the city three months ago. Since then, you've acquired a new tailor, a cook from the south, and a mistress who favors the scent of gardenias. You fear someone is trying to poison you, and you are seeking the blessing of the Church to maintain your hold on Sirenza. You continue to slay those who stand against you or speak ill of your governance. As you will doubtless slay me, for speaking so to you. But you know very well that I despise you; there would be no point to dissembling now."

He sheathed his sword and clapped his hands together, laughing outright. I took a long, deep breath to steady myself. I had been certain he was just playing with me and that he was going to kill me whatever I said. He still might, I reminded myself. But his cheeks were flushed, his hazel eyes bright, and he continued to laugh, waggling one gloved finger at me. "I hope that's not the manner you affect during all readings. Hardly theatrical, my dear. But all very true, except for that last bit. I will not slay you."

The captain rose and departed the wagon. I sat,

taking great deep breaths to calm myself. I was dimly aware of Ubaldo's voice close beside the wagon. "Yes, my lord, of course, yes, the finest in all the lands." The stream of fawning affirmations went on. Niccolo's light tenor did not carry so well, so I learned nothing more.

By the time I had divested myself of my costume and come outside, the crowds had dispersed. Coso and Cristo were entertaining a dozen or so, including my father. Of Ubaldo and Niccolo there was no sign. I went to Father.

"Where's Ubaldo?" I asked.

"He went away with Captain Niccolo. Did you see, Nata? He was still wearing the boots I made him. Remember those? Such beauties, that fine red suede, and the carvings on the black leather. He always wanted the best, that one. He's a powerful man now, you know. I hope he was pleased with his fortune."

"He was." Why he had been, I did not know. I was just glad that he was gone.

The Saints heeded my request, or perhaps I was lucky. Ubaldo returned a short time later, greatly agitated, but flushed with good humor. "Coso, Cristo, get the wagon packed. We leave tonight."

"Tonight? After a single day?" Cristo asked.

"We've bigger meats to feast on," Ubaldo said, grinning. "We leave for Doma this night."

"Doma? Why Doma? Why now?" Coso asked. I was

glad he had, for I was as puzzled as he, but less willing to risk Ubaldo's anger. His moods were mercurial, and these sunny skies might hold hidden thunder.

"There's work in Doma, a special opportunity. For all of us, but especially for you, girl." He jerked his bearded chin at me. "And you'd best be grateful for it. You've been pulling in precious little coin. I should toss you and the old man on the side of the road, where I found you. But if you do well at this job, perhaps I'll reconsider that."

CHAPTER

5

I T TOOK US TWO WEEKS to reach Doma, keeping a fast pace and rising each morning in the dim gray light long before true dawn. Franca didn't much like it, nor did I. Ubaldo was being distressingly close-lipped about his great plan and the big work he had for me.

I tried to find out what I could from other travelers. We had stopped so that Ubaldo could drink from a spring off the roadway. I gave up my own chance for a drink to chat with a pair of young men who had stopped to take their midday meal. I had heard one of them mention Doma.

"Yes, we've come from there," the elder told me, leaning back against an empty pushcart that smelled faintly of fennel and sage. "Sold a great lot of our sausages to old Giolli in the merchants' quarter. Fine city, terrible shame about the prince."

"What about the prince?" I asked.

"Well, you know, how he can't—" the younger man started to say.

"You traveling to Doma yourselves?" the other man interrupted. "You some sort of traveling players?"

"Yes, juggling, knife throwing, and fortunes told," I said. "But what about the prince?"

"Fortunes?" the older man repeated. "You're a fortune-teller? And you're going *toward* Doma?"

His emphasis on the word "toward" sent a shiver along my spine.

"Come along, girl, we're leaving!" Ubaldo shouted from the direction of the wagons.

"Please," I begged the two sausage-sellers, "what do you mean? Why shouldn't a fortune-teller go to Doma? Aren't they welcome there?"

"Oh, aye, they welcome them gladly, but—"

His words were cut off by the thunder of Ubaldo's voice in my ear. "Now, girl, or I'll tie you to the wheels next time!" He seized the back of my gown and dragged me bodily toward the wagon.

I HAD LEARNED little more by the time we reached Doma. We approached from the rolling hills to the south, which afforded a magnificent view of the valley and the city at its heart. A sturdy wall prickling with watchtowers encircled a profusion of brown and golden buildings. A river divided the city in two; several large bridges spanned the blue waters. At the very center rose a great golden building that could only be the palace.

The river widened into a lake as it passed out from the city proper. Our road wound along its banks toward the gate. Guards in crisp white and scarlet met us there, inquiring as to our business.

Ubaldo plucked me out of the rear of the blue wagon, where he had sent me to put on my costume. He propelled me before one of the guards as I tried vainly to straighten my starry headdress. "My name is Ubaldo," he announced. "This is the prophetess Fortunata of the All-Knowing Eye. We've come to see the queen."

"What?" I gasped. "The queen? Are you mad?"

Ubaldo tightened his grip on my arm. "Hold your tongue, girl."

Ubaldo's pronouncement had had a strange effect on the guards. I didn't think they would have noticed my outburst even if I had screamed it. One of them darted off into the tower beside the gate. Another was shouting orders, and still more were clearing the way before us.

"My men will escort you to the palace. The queen awaits you," said the guard, "and by the Saints, may you be the one." He looked at me with wide, desperate eyes, unnerving in such an otherwise capable and martial man.

I was trying to maintain my composure, but there were so many questions whirling in my head now. What did he mean by "the one"? And an audience with the queen? What was Ubaldo up to? Belatedly, I wondered if there was a way I could keep Father out of it. But the ranks of soldiers had surrounded both wagons in a phalanx of scarlet.

Ubaldo waved Coso forward with the air of a captain on parade. He pulled me up with him into the blue wagon, and we passed through the gates and into the city. There were crowds watching us eagerly, drawn thick as flies to honey. Our guards had to push them back. They were cheering and shouting, but I could make out no words.

"Ubaldo, what's going on?"

"You heard the man. We're going to see the queen. You've a fortune to tell."

I was glad I was sitting already, for otherwise I would have toppled over. "You want me to tell the queen her fortune? She'll never see us! And why should she?"

"The queen of Doma has a call out to any fortune-teller in the lands. You play this smart, and I'll see you and your father get a share of the earnings. You hear me?"

I swallowed against the dryness in my throat. It must be serious for Ubaldo to actually offer money. "The queen of Doma wants me to read her fortune?" I repeated. My hands trembled. I had dreamed of prophesying for royalty, but this was no dream. I feared it might actually be a nightmare. Curse Ubaldo for not telling me his plan!

"No, her son's. The prince's. And you'll give him a good one, by all the seven Hells."

Oh, Allessandra, I thought, where are you? I would need all her tricks to get through this with my head intact. Did I dare lie to a prince, to a queen? Spin them some golden floss of a future out of nothing but the few straws I could gather? I could refuse, but what would Ubaldo do then?

My agitated thoughts were interrupted by our abrupt halt. We had reached the palace. It stretched up twice as tall as any other building nearby, the bright golden dome of the central rotunda glimmering in the morning sunlight. Two square towers flanked the dome, and between them ran the great stone edifice under which we had stopped. A vast open plaza surrounded the palace, swirling with pigeons and people, the latter held back by rows of stern, red-garbed guards.

The gathered crowds were muttering and buzzing with chatter. I perked my ears for something that might help me make sense of this strange situation. Bits of conversation stood out here and there. *So long since the king passed on. . . . Princess Donata stands ready. . . . Edicts will never be fulfilled. . . . Tired of waiting. . . . Doma suffers. . . . Will this be the one?*

I looked up at the palace, ornate with carved cherubs and images of the Saints trailing stone leaves and fruits, as elaborate as one of Zia Rosa's wedding cakes. How I wished then to be back in Valenzia ogling treats at her bakery, my only fear whether I could talk Zia Rosa into giving me an extra cherry-almond tart. But here I was, about to try to talk a prince into believing my lies.

A set of wide, shallow steps led up to the double doors, which stood open, flanked by more of the scarlet guards. A balcony swept out directly above us. Someone was up there, a young man, I thought, craning my neck to look up at him. His hair glinted gold as the dome itself. I had the sudden feeling he was looking at me, though he was too distant to make out clearly. Then he turned and retreated into the palace.

Even Ubaldo seemed discomfited by our surroundings. He covered it up by shouting at Coso and Cristo to watch the horses and wagon, but his face was flushed and his bald head slick with sweat. I took advantage of his distraction to slip down from the blue wagon. I wanted Father with me, whatever happened. I did not trust Ubaldo one jot, and though he claimed we were welcome here, I wasn't planning to take any risks.

"Nata, dear, what is the meaning of all this?" Father whispered as two guards appeared on either side of us.

"I don't know, Papa. Ubaldo's up to something; he says I'm to read the fortune of the prince."

"Well, my child, if anyone can do so, it will be you. You've the magic, I've seen it."

Lies and trickery. Not magic. But would a prince know any better than a shepherd or a farmer? I'd told fortunes for clerics and sages, with none ever questioning the truth of it. I gulped down a deep breath and took tight hold of Father's hand.

Our scarlet guards escorted Ubaldo, Father, and me up the stairs to the great double doors of the palace. Another man in scarlet stood there, a reedy fellow with a puckered scar along the line of his chin. Though he looked to be twice as old as our fresh-faced guards, his movements were even sharper, his back straighter. In his eyes I found no hint of the excitement or expectation that bubbled all around us.

"So this is another one?" he said simply as we surmounted the last step.

"Yes, Captain Ribisi," the guard at my right said. "Now at last we will have the Edicts fulfilled!"

"We'll see about that," Captain Ribisi said drily.

He led us along a wide hall paneled in dark wood. I had to keep tugging Father's hand, as he would stop at every painting and bronze to ogle, and there were many.

"A dozen Bragellis already!" Father said. He pulled me aside toward an alcove housing a life-sized bronze of a maiden seated upon an ornate chair, with a courtly knight kneeling before her. "And look! Nata! The slipper! Do you see it?"

I saw, though I had to blink to be sure of it. The knight was kneeling not simply in obeisance, as I had first thought. He held, in his bronze hands, a single golden leather shoe, encrusted with jewels. The maiden had one slender bronze foot lifted and held out, in the act of slipping it into the shoe.

"Is it one of yours, Papa?" I asked.

He shook his head, sadly. "No, even when the fairies still granted me their magic, I could not have made such a slipper. Perhaps my own papa, in his prime, might have dreamed such a thing."

A small plaque was affixed at the base of the statue. I squinted to read it. *Queen Rosetta receives the gift of the doge of Valenzia.*

Father was still gazing raptly at the slipper.

"Papa, could it be? You told me that story once about the doge buying the slippers right off Grandmo—"

"You can gawk at the art later, old man," Ubaldo said, shoving both of us along. "The girl has work to do."

"Stop," said a sibilant voice from deeper within the alcove. Captain Ribisi glanced back at the figure that emerged from the shadows behind the statue, then raised one hand crisply. Our escort halted.

"Princess Donata," he greeted the woman in a

carefully colorless voice. "I'm afraid your nephew is expecting these . . . guests. We must proceed."

"Now, my dear captain, surely my nephew can wait a bit longer. You know he's used to it. And I would very much like to meet our newest candidate."

She stepped out into the light of the hall, but she was like a piece of shadow herself, lithe and dark and seeming to hide any number of unknown dangers. Her gown was a rich midnight blue, and a matching scarf covered her fair hair. She swept her gaze over all of us, settling last on me. I straightened my headdress, wondering what exactly she meant by "candidate."

"This one's but a girl herself," Princess Donata said. "And yet she has the Sight? She is the one who will reveal our prince's fortune to him, that he might fulfill the Edicts and become king at last?"

"Yes, my lady," Ubaldo said, clasping his thick hands together and ducking his head as he spoke. "We heard of the queen's call, and if it's true visions she wants, Fortunata here will give them. She's got the Sight, I swear it on the Saints, every last one. Why, just last week she foretold a great flood in Sirenza; without her word, there would have been hundreds perished."

"A flood was it?" The woman arched her fine golden brows.

"Yes, and the scarlet fever, when it came to Valenzia. And she's foretold hundreds of weddings. And she can summon spirits of the departed, for an extra fee, of course." He licked his lips and grinned broadly.

I gritted my teeth. Any fool could tell Ubaldo was lying, and this woman was no fool. But she simply smiled. "Very well then, Fortunata, you are all I could hope for. I am glad to hear that our city's future lies in such good hands. Go on, Captain, take the seer to her fate. Though I am sure one of her power must already know what lies ahead." As the captain led us off down the hall, I could hear Princess Donata chuckling.

I was more relieved than nervous when we reached a great white door emblazoned with a golden crown. At last I would have some answers, or so I hoped.

Captain Ribisi led the way into the crowded audience chamber. The buzz of conversation died away instantly. His boots rang out loud as cathedral bells as he crossed the open expanse of the hall toward a dais at the far end. Ranks of courtiers in rich silks and velvets lined the sides; all eyes were upon us. Ubaldo, Father, and I followed the captain, herded along by our ever-present coterie of guards. Two tall gilt chairs stood atop the dais, but only one was occupied.

The woman seated there was pale and slightly plump, with a face curved and soft as a swan's feather, though tracked by lines of care and worry. She looked as if she had been crying.

Captain Ribisi bowed so low his nose touched the

knee of his bent leg, then swept up smoothly. "Your Highness, I present the All-Knowing Fortunata, Mistress of the Unknown, who has heeded your call and comes to grant her wisdom in our time of need." I could have sworn that the captain smirked slightly over that pronouncement, but it was hard to tell under his large gray mustache.

Ubaldo tweaked my elbow, so I stepped forward, attempting a curtsy. My feet felt as if they were encased in lead.

"You claim to have the Sight?" asked the queen. "You swear that you come here truthfully, in good faith, and that the words you speak will be genuine prophecy?"

I froze. My lips were parted, and I had taken in the breath to speak, but I was suddenly speechless. Beneath my starry headdress, beads of sweat matted my hair. Dared I lie to a queen, before dozens of worthy witnesses? Yet if I denied it, what would Ubaldo do to me, to Father?

"My daughter is all those things, and more," said a voice from beside me. I turned to see Father, hands clasped, blinking through his great thick spectacles at the queen. His hands trembled slightly, but his voice was firm. "She has been granted the magic of sight; she truly does see what will be. I have seen those to whom she has granted comfort and peace in the knowledge of what shall come to pass."

I couldn't help but smile. I would have believed him

myself, if I didn't know better. Father always did have the strength to believe in anything. Just not himself.

"You swear this? It is a matter of great importance. The Edicts must be observed. And we have been misled so often. . . ." The queen trailed off, dabbing at her eyes with a lace-edged handkerchief.

"Oh, yes, I swear it on the soul of my dear, departed wife. By all the Saints. On my own life, I swear it." Father looked at me with shining eyes. I felt my own eyes smart.

Father's pronouncement sent the crowds of courtiers into a buzz of conversation, though it did not disguise the grumbling "hmph" from Captain Ribisi.

"Very well." The queen turned to me. Did she expect me to prophesy then and there? The reassurance of Father's faith in me slipped away with the hammering pulse of my heart. Then she spoke again, and the courtiers fell silent. "Our noble city of Doma has flourished for generations under her kings and queens. It was the first of our line who set down the Edicts that have guided us all these years. The Edicts are the core of Doma, and they must be followed, lest ruin and devastation be visited upon us by the Saints. Read now the Fifth Edict, Jacopo," she commanded a rotund man with ink-stained fingers who stood at the edge of the dais.

He shuffled the sheets of parchment in his hands and gave several harrumphing coughs. Drawing himself up impressively, he read aloud. "'When it shall come time for a Prince to ascend to the Throne, he must embark first upon his Great Quest, and shall in due course rescue, with strength of arms and purity of heart, a fair and noble Princess beset at that time by Dire Peril. Upon the Triumphant Return of the Prince, he shall ask for the Hand of the Princess in Marriage under the Blessing of the Saints, that she may join him as Queen.'"

My confused thoughts whirled like a flock of unsettled birds. There had been no mention of a prophecy in the Edict. Where did I fit into this puzzle? I struggled to remain calm. I had to pay close attention now. My success could depend on the smallest detail, the hints that might reveal what the queen was looking for. The clerk Jacopo stepped back, furling the papers. To my relief, the queen spoke again.

"For generations we have followed the Edicts faithfully. All the rulers of Doma have found their consorts in pursuance of those words. My dear Giovanni rescued me from the cruel imprisonment of a witch's tower, in my homeland of Utto. Now, it is time for our son, Prince Leonato, to step forth and take his place upon the throne of his father. But he may not be crowned king until the Edict is fulfilled."

I followed this so far, but still did not see where I or my fortunes would fit in. My heart hammered. I felt as if I stood ready to run a footrace, sweat slick on my palms, excitement and fear shivering in my limbs.

"But the Saints have chosen to test us. For it has been five years since the death of our beloved King Giovanni, and in that time we have found no Princess in Dire Peril to satisfy the Fifth Edict. That is why you have been summoned here, seer." She turned to Jacopo again. "Read the Sixth Edict."

The clerk obliged, after additional shuffling of papers. " 'If such a Princess in Dire Peril be not readily apparent, the Prince shall consult a True Seer, and receive his fortune, which shall tell of the Princess and where she may be found. The Prince shall proclaim the Prophecy to the people, and its Truth shall ring from his lips without falter. He shall then set forth and fulfill his destiny.' "

"Now then, we await your prophecy," said the queen, nodding to me.

The thrumming of my heartbeat was so loud I thought they all must hear it as they stared at me in the silence that followed. But this was no time for nerves. I had prophesied for Captain Niccolo, with his sword to my throat. I could do this. Somehow, I must produce a Princess in Dire Peril. They were all watching me, waiting for this fabled prophecy. I swallowed against the dryness that threatened to choke me.

"I, Fortunata the All-Knowing, now part the veils cast over what may be, and look forward into the future." I began with my standard flummery, which gave me a few more precious moments to think. I knew of no princesses in peril, dire or otherwise. But I did know a whole city that was. "I see a city. It floats upon the river, its very streets are water. But the water runs with blood, under the cruel villain who has slain so many. He holds the city in his iron fist, and the people suffer. There, the princess is there. In Sirenza, in Dire Peril under the threat of the Bloody Captain."

I took a long, shaky breath. There had to be any number of eligible young ladies in that city who were in dire peril. One of them would do. And if Captain Niccolo was killed in the process, all the better, as far as I was concerned. I had given them a nice, simple prophecy and now I could go. Perhaps in a few days this horrible fluttering in my belly would calm down.

"But the princesses of Sirenza were slain—that is what the rumors say," said one of the courtiers.

I forced myself to unlock my clenched fists and smooth out the robes I'd been clutching. I wanted to turn and run, before I got any deeper into this dark wood of lies. But I had come too far now to turn back.

"The Bloody Captain did seek to slay all the royal family of Sirenza," I said. "But the princess escaped. She was hidden among the people." That should do it. The prince would probably get hold of the first pretty girl he found. I didn't suppose she would object to becoming a princess.

"Oh, great seer, how shall the princess be known?" asked the queen.

Vainly I searched my mind for something suitable. What had I gotten myself into? Panic champed on the edges of my thoughts. I pushed it back. I had to do this. If I could make this fortune work, it might earn Father and me the coin we needed to leave Ubaldo forever. I stared into space, hoping I looked suitably enigmatic as my mind raced desperately for an answer. Then Allessandra's advice came back to me. She had always said to use what is at hand. People will more readily accept a fortune if it is composed of things they see every day. I remembered the bronze from the hall.

"The slippers," I said. "The golden slippers of Queen Rosetta. They will fit only a True Princess, a girl suited to wed her grandson." There had to be some girls in Sirenza who would fit them. As long as the prince found one of them, my fortune would suffice.

There was an appreciative oohing and ahhing from the crowd of courtiers, but the queen looked puzzled. "The slippers?" she repeated.

I'd said something wrong. I swallowed the lump that had lodged in my throat. "The slippers that were gifted her by the doge of Valenzia." Curse it! I sounded like I was asking a question, not delivering mystical truth from beyond.

"But we have only the one! The other was lost, years ago, in the Black Wood. Stolen by the Witch of the Black Wood, so my husband said."

"Then it shall be recovered," I said quickly. By the seven Hells! Why had I used the plural? I had seen only one, but I assumed. . . . I raised my hand to wipe my sweaty brow. Belatedly, I turned the gesture into a sort of theatrical wave, as if I were sweeping away the fog that cloaked my vision. I couldn't give up. If the prince had to go off into the Black Wood for a bit, that would only enhance the quest. "Yes, the prince must recover the stolen slipper from the Witch of the Black Wood."

"But, how shall the witch be defeated?" asked the queen. "She has magics upon her that will guard her from the blades of mortal folk."

Yes, I thought, a witch had little to fear from mortals. Because witches, like fortunes and fairies, were nothing but lies. You couldn't harm something that didn't exist. I struggled to think of an answer, the thrum of my heart loud in my ears. Ubaldo stirred beside me, a low warning rumble. I bit down on the furious words I would have spoken had we not been standing before the queen. Ubaldo had no right to be angry, bringing me here without a hint of what was to come. If he'd told me his plan, I might have concocted a better story. But here I was, trying to produce a believable prophecy to defeat a witch that didn't exist, with my throat dry as kindling. Ubaldo shifted and surreptitiously pinched my arm. I gritted my teeth. Enough. I could do this. I was good at it. Even Ubaldo knew that. I would finish this.

I said the first thing that came to mind. "The prince shall find a weapon to defeat the witch in a village three days' travel to the . . . east," I improvised. "He shall ride forth from Doma tomorrow, upon a snow-white steed, panoplied for his great quest. He shall face great danger, and terrible trials, yet his courage and honor shall guide him true, and he shall return to Doma with the True Princess at his side. That is the wisdom of the All-Knowing Eye."

I dipped in a rough curtsy, holding my breath. I had gotten a trifle carried away at the end there. But now it was done, for good or ill. The roiling tension rushed out from me, leaving my limbs shaky and my belly sour. There was a long pause, during which the only sound was the scratch of a quill on parchment. With a twinge of foreboding, I saw that Jacopo the clerk had been recording my words.

The queen smiled, a trifle fixedly. "The thanks of all Doma to you, Fortunata, for this prophecy. My son shall make ready to depart on the morn."

A halfhearted wave of clapping rose from the crowd of courtiers. A glance from the queen provoked a few additional cheers, but for the most part, the onlookers remained remarkably unenthusiastic. Well, I thought, slightly offended, it was the best I could do on short notice. Hadn't they heard the part about the witch? That was worth at least a few huzzahs.

I steadied myself with a deep breath. Ubaldo had better hold to his word and give Father and me our share of the earnings. I never wanted to go through this again. Thank the Saints it was over.

"And now," the queen said, "you will wish to refresh yourself before embarking on the journey."

"The journey?" I repeated dumbly.

"Of course. You will accompany my son on his quest, and see that it comes to pass as you have foretold," the queen said. "Your father has sworn that you possess the True Sight, but so too have others before you. Doma does not look well upon those who swear falsely, and to do so before the queen means death."

"D-death?" I stammered.

"Be at peace, Fortunata, for if you truly have the Sight, there is no reason to fear. Your father will be our guest, and granted warm lodging and plentiful food, until the time your prophecy comes to pass."

"And if it doesn't?"

The queen snapped her fingers, and Jacopo scuttled forward to hand her the parchment he had been inscribing. She glanced it over, then held it aloft.

"As I said, to swear falsely means death. That is our law. Here stands a record of your prophecy for my son. If this fortune does not come to pass, your father will die."

CHAPTER

6

I LOOKED AROUND Father's prison bleakly. It was certainly no stinking dungeon, nor a high, remote tower. It was a perfectly comfortable, well-appointed chamber, the walls hung with rich tapestries, the huge wooden bed hung with red velvet, the wide windows letting in streams of afternoon sunlight, with heavy drapes standing ready against the chill of evening. A silver tray held a roast fowl, fried cabbage, and a plump almond pastry. It was, in fact, one of the finest rooms I had ever seen. But it was still a prison.

"Look, Nata, this is a de Nussi, here, in my very room!" Father had his nose pressed up against a painting of the ascension of Saint Rosa that hung beside the bed.

"Father, you can't stay here," I said. "We must find a way to escape. They're going to execute you!"

He turned from the painting, brow furrowed. "Execute me? Whatever for?"

"My fortune, if it doesn't come true, Papa, the queen said—"

Father chuckled, waving aside my fears. "Oh, Nata, it will come true. You've the True Sight, just as I said. That prince of theirs will have his princess back here by next Saints' Day, I'd wager. Not nearly long enough for me to tire of this beautiful room. Ah, how your mother would have loved it. She always had a hankering for velvet."

I went to the window and pushed past the drapes to peer down. Very far down. The people milling about the plaza were small as dolls, and the pigeons mere specks. There was no escape that way. While Father continued to exclaim over the thickly woven rug and finely crafted chairs, I marched to the door and threw it open. Two stern guards regarded me, stiff at attention on either side of the doorway.

I turned back, and threw myself down on the couch Father was admiring, cradling my head in my hands. It was no use. My horrible, false fortune would never come true, and Father was going to pay the price for my foolishness.

The couch creaked as he sat beside me. "Nata, dear, don't worry. I told you, I'll be fine."

I couldn't bear to look up, to see his faithful gaze. He had believed in me, and I had let him down utterly.

Father patted my shoulder. "I know your fortune will come to pass."

His words broke my descent into despair, tossing me the slenderest of ropes. I raised my head and covered his hand with my own, giving it a gentle squeeze. "You're right, Papa. It will come true." I continued on, as much to reassure myself as my father. I would need all the Saints smiling on me to pull this off. "Then we'll be free of Ubaldo. We can go back to Valenzia, or any other city you like. We'll buy a house of our own, with velvet drapes and a great big workshop for you. It will be so fine you won't need magic."

"You've all our magic now, Nata," he said. "But look where it's gotten us. Into the palace of a queen!"

And into a whole stew of trouble. My frail, newborn hope didn't cloud my eyes to that fact. I had no magic. But I would get us out of this with what I did have. My wits and my cleverness had earned me, or rather Ubaldo, a pig's weight of guilders. Now they were all I had to get us out of this mess. If Father's life depended on it, well then, I would have to *make* my fortune come true.

I LEFT FATHER happily admiring the porcelain ewers in the washroom and decided to set out in search of anything that might help me. I had some thought of going to see the slipper in the grand hall. I had foretold that the prince must recover a matching shoe from a witch I didn't believe existed in a forest so vast none knew its farthest boundary. The real slipper was probably rotting under a dozen years' worth of mulch by now. Perhaps I could have a duplicate made.

As I stepped into the hall outside Father's chamber, what little optimism I had disappeared. A third red-garbed figure had joined the guards in the hall.

"Hello, Captain Ribisi," I said, attempting politeness.

He inclined his gray head. "Mistress Fortunata. Don't tell me some vision draws you forth?" The twitch of his lips told how little he believed that.

"No, ah, I only wished to get a bit of fresh air. And I hoped to see some of your beautiful palace. Before I leave. With the prince. On the quest." My halting words only made his lips twitch again.

"You seem very certain you will be leaving."

"Of course. As the queen said, once the prince makes his proclamation of the prophecy, I'm to accompany him on the quest. Unless I've misunderstood?" I tried to hide the excitement in my voice. Perhaps Papa and I could escape together, while the prince was off searching for a nonexistent witch.

"Yes, that is what the Edicts decree. You should know, however, that you are not the first so-called seer to come to Doma."

"I had heard something of that," I admitted.

"In that case, you might also have heard that every one of them failed to deliver a true prophecy."

Curiosity overwhelmed my attempts to appear remote and all-knowing. "Did any of them come close?"

"None of them even made it out of the city."

My mind whirled, trying to find sense in this. What could stop every single prophesied quest from leaving the city? All that was supposed to happen before we departed was that business about the prince proclaiming the truth of the prophecy to the people. I realized my mouth was open, and shut it.

Just then a patter of footsteps announced a breathless page, come to call Captain Ribisi away on some other matter.

"Enjoy your tour of the palace, Mistress Fortunata," he said, before turning to follow the page.

Saints be praised. I sped off down the hallway, eager to be out of the man's cold glare. But I couldn't escape the chill his warning had cast over me. There was something I did not know, and I felt sure it was going to be trouble. How many other seers had come before me? What had become of them? Why had they failed? All I could hope was that my exploration might yield more clues.

It took me quite some time to find my way down the numerous stairways and winding passages back to the main hall. The servants were bustling about in such a state I did not dare to ask directions. Besides, why would a true seer need something as simple as directions?

Before long I lost all sense of where I might be. I found myself in a wide, windowless corridor lit by braziers. It terminated at a large door, similar to so many others I had passed through already. I sighed and debated going back, but decided to at least see what was on the other side of this door. With any luck, it would be the sweeping staircase down to the ground floor of the palace.

I shoved the heavy door open. There was no staircase. Instead I found a richly furnished room, all violet and gold. It was quite dark, but the single shaft of light from the one window showed me something of great interest: a large painting covering nearly all of the facing wall.

I slipped into the room, pulling the door closed behind me, then tiptoed over to the painting. A richly garbed lady upon a pure white horse galloped through a tangle of dark trees. She rode sidesaddle, trailing her long, pale gown over the flanks of the horse. One foot peeked out from the hem, clad in a golden slipper. The other foot was bare. Behind her, flying through the dark trees with her ragged black sleeves stretched out like wings, came the witch. Her face was slightly green and speckled with warts. In one clawlike hand she held the second gold slipper.

I searched the painting for clues as to where this might have taken place, but found none. Disappointed, I was turning to depart when I heard voices outside. I looked around at the rest of the room for the first time, and my heart jumped. It was a personal chamber, a lady's, judging by the array of brushes and jeweled hair ornaments laid out on the toilette table nearby.

"I have it, Princess, as you asked," said a man outside.

"Silence, you fool!" said a woman's voice. "Not out here!"

Princess Donata! I looked wildly for a way out, but found none. There was another door, but it was on the far side of the room. I couldn't reach it in time. I darted instead for the window and pulled the heavy drape in front of me just as the door creaked open. I begged the Saints not to let her discover me.

Footsteps shuffled across the thick carpets, then the door shut once more. "Now, then, where is it?"

"Here, my princess, a fair copy, down to the last letter." I frowned, recognizing the voice of Jacopo, the fat clerk from the audience hall that morning. What was he doing meeting clandestinely with Princess Donata?

"And this is exactly what she said?"

"Yes, Your Highness, every word of the prophecy."

She snickered. I could hear the rustle of parchment being unfurled. "No more prophecy than any of the others. I doubt we need interfere with this one to gain our purpose. Look at this rubbish. Witches and the Black Wood. Mother's ridiculous slippers. And a princess from Sirenza?" She gave a sharp bark of laughter. "The Bloody Captain's no fool. There's not a girl alive in Sirenza with even a drop of royal blood."

"But what if—"

"Oh, I will be prepared. If there is the merest hint that the little fool's prophecy might come to pass, it will be dealt with. But I doubt my nephew will make it out of the city, and I won't have to lift a finger. Not with all this nonsense about slippers and Sirenza and snow-white steeds." She chuckled again, though I couldn't understand what was so amusing.

"And then you will be queen," said Jacopo silkily.

"And those who have helped me shall be richly rewarded." I could almost hear the clink of golden coins in her voice. "Now go. Leave me."

Jacopo departed, trailing a flood of obsequious compliments. Princess Donata, alas, gave no sign of leaving. She was probably plotting and scheming ways to foil my fortune while my legs grew stiff and my nose itched with dust from her curtains.

I heard steps again, moving away. I risked a peek through a gap in the drapes. Princess Donata stood at the far end of the room, rummaging in a tall armoire. I watched, one hand pinching my nose against the threat of a sneeze. At last Princess Donata passed out of sight through the smaller door on the other side of the room.

Before I could think better of it, I had scrambled out from my hiding place and darted across the room. Throwing open the main doors, I burst out into the hall. I did not look back. My stomach felt cold, and despair gnawed at my heart. Now not only must I make my own extravagant fortune come true, but I must do so against the efforts of a power-hungry princess who wanted the throne for herself. What had I done to deserve this fate? Were the Saints punishing me for all the false fortunes I had given? Well, curse the Saints, then, for I had done what I must to keep us alive.

I burst around a corner and collided with someone. The impact sent me staggering back. My long fortune-telling robes wound around my feet, tripping me. I blinked up at the person I had run into.

He looked like the statues of Marco the Fair, most beautiful of all the Saints. Cornsilk yellow hair lay in curls like gold coins across his sun-tinged brow. For a moment I feared the Saints had sent one of their own to punish me for my curse. But this Saint did not look angry. I stared into brilliant green eyes that turned all the world quiet and reverent as a forest glade in the sun. I realized I was staring.

"Your pardon, please," I gasped, scrambling to rise.

The Saint extended a hand to help me up.

"Your headdress, miss," said someone else. Captain Ribisi held out my star-spangled cap with its trailing black gauze, now torn in several places.

The Saint's eyes grew wider, looking between me and the headdress.

"My prince, this is the girl—excuse me, miss," Captain Ribisi said, with an exaggerated politeness I did not care for. "This is the latest seer to prophesy how you will fulfill the Edicts. I trust, Mistress Fortunata, that you see the future more clearly than you see who is coming toward you along the hall."

Prince. The word penetrated my addled brain at last, and I realized who I had run into. He certainly looked the part. I could not have invented a more fitting hero for this endeavor had I tried. I clapped my headdress back on and tucked the veil to disguise the rents. I had never felt less convincing in my role as Fortunata of the All-Knowing Eye. But Prince Leonato smiled, and something in the curve of his lips untied the knot in my belly.

"Perhaps sh-sh-sh—" the prince began, but his lips twisted, and the word would not come. I glanced at Captain Ribisi, and for the first time he looked something other than grim or ironic. His attention was fixed upon Prince Leonato, a crease between his brows.

A tinge of pink colored the prince's cheeks, whether

from embarrassment or effort I could not tell. "Sh-sh—" he tried again and finally blurted out, "she had a vision that I was s-s-searching for her." He took a deep breath upon finishing the statement.

The deep gully between Captain Ribisi's brows relaxed once the prince had finished speaking. "My prince, you must not put too much faith in these seers. You know what has happened before. We have not had a true prophecy yet."

"The problem might not be with the s-s—" Prince Leonato abandoned whatever he was trying to say. He was still as beautiful as Saint Marco, but I had never seen an image of the Saint looking this miserable.

"My prince, you must not doubt—" Captain Ribisi began. Then he seemed to recall I was there too, and left the sentence unfinished.

"So, Your Highness," I said, "was there something you wanted to ask me?"

Prince Leonato looked like the last thing in the world he wanted to do just then was open his mouth, but he nodded.

Another guard came hurrying up the hall. Captain Ribisi stepped aside to speak with him, leaving me alone with the prince. Leonato tugged briefly on the high collar of his coat. A sheen of sweat glistened on his brow, dampening his golden curls.

"Prophetess, do you really s-s-see me being crowned?" he asked, then hurried to add, "It's not that I want to be. I s-s-saw how hard it was for Father." The flush on Leonato's cheeks deepened with each faltering word, but he pressed on. "But the people s-s-say the land is cursed now, without a leader. The crops are poor, there's been s-s-sickness and unrest. I want to make things better, but I've failed s-s-s—" He grimaced, then started over. "I've failed every time, with my s-s-stupid s-s-stuttering. Mother and the captain s-s-say the prophecies have been false. But I know the truth. It's me. I wasn't s-s-supposed to be king."

The poor boy was pinker now than those ridiculous sausage boots I'd tricked Niccolo into buying back in Valenzia. His desperation made my heart ache. I nearly reached out to him, to take his hand and tell him that this ridiculous Edict business had nothing to do with being a good king. But the prophecy was a matter of life and death to me now. *The Prince shall proclaim the Prophecy to the people, and its Truth shall ring from his lips without falter.* The words of the Edict reverberated like funeral bells in my mind.

"Don't worry, Prince Leonato. You will make the pronouncement of *this* quest without faltering." I wasn't sure how, but if Father was to live, I would have to find a way. Besides, the prince needed the hope of a good fortune as much as any penniless singer or struggling young lover.

"If I can't fulfill the Edicts," he said, "my aunt Donata will take the crown. And sh-sh-she—"

"Prince Leonato," Captain Ribisi said, rejoining us, "I am afraid there's some trouble concerning the prophecy."

"What is it?" I asked, almost glad for the interruption. Whatever it was, it had to be less of a problem than the prince's stutter.

"It concerns the prince's *snow-white* steed," Ribisi answered, giving sardonic emphasis to the phrase. "I fear the stable master has no such beast. Black, roan, dun, piebald. But no white horses. Could the prophetess have been mistaken?" He turned cold eyes on me. "Bad luck, perhaps?"

Saints! What had possessed me to say it was a snow-white steed? Just my luck to have chosen the one color not in the royal stables. Then I remembered what I had overheard in Princess Donata's chamber. *I doubt my nephew will make it out of the city.* Bad luck, or design?

"The prince will ride out on a snow-white steed tomorrow," I said, pulling myself up tall and straightening my glittering robes. "I have foreseen it. But only a special beast is suited for a great quest such as this. It will not be found within the royal stables, but somewhere within the city itself. We shall go and seek it out." There must be one white horse somewhere in Doma, I thought. I would just have to search until I found it.

THERE WAS INDEED one white horse in Doma, and only one. I said it was a special beast, but I had not expected this. It was a huge, brutish creature, swaybacked and sullen. It even bit me when I tried to feed it a carrot. The miller who owned it was loath to part with it, but yielded in the end when Prince Leonato produced a heavy sack of guilders. It was enough to have bought a dozen fine stallions, rather than this rundown monster, which had the unlikely name of Snowdrop.

But if the gelding was nothing else, he was white. A bit dirty, yes, but white from hoof to snout underneath it. Prince Leonato immediately sent for a half-dozen stable hands to tend to the horse and clean it up. Finding Snowdrop seemed to have raised the prince's spirits, or at least had distracted him from the prospect of tomorrow's proclamation.

I was not so lucky. I was exhausted by the events of the day, but my hardest tasks still lay before me. It wouldn't matter if Snowdrop were the purest white steed in all the lands if the prince could not declare the words of my prophecy on the morrow without stuttering. I needed to find a solution, and there was very little time left to do so. While at the stables, Captain Ribisi announced the need for a mount for me. I told him about Franca and asked that she be brought for me to ride. If things went poorly, perhaps Papa and I could escape on her sturdy gray back. If all went smoothly, maybe I could keep her when this was over. If nothing else, it would prevent Ubaldo from selling her while I was gone. The guards returned a short time later, leading Franca. They also brought another, less welcome, addition.

Ubaldo bowed his bald head to Leonato. "Ah, there you are, Fortunata. Keeping company with the prince himself, I see. Your Highness, it's an honor."

"And you are, s-s-sir?" Leonato asked.

"Ubaldo, Your Highness. The girl, the prophetess, rather, she's mine." I stirred at that, and Leonato glanced in my direction. Ubaldo went on. "Her and the old man. It was I brought them here to aid you."

"Then I am most s-s-s-sincerely obliged," Leonato said, color leaping to his face as he fought to speak. Ubaldo, of course, was too self-interested to notice the prince's stutter.

"So, we depart on the morrow, then," Ubaldo said, looking over the fine horses that stood in the nearby stalls. He thrust Franca's lead rope into my hands. "Here's my donkey, which the girl is welcome to borrow for the journey. I'll be needing a mount of my own. These are some fine beasts you have here."

"You're coming with us?" I said, my fingers tightening on the rope. I started to step away, trying to pull Franca after me.

"Of course," he said, setting a meaty hand on my arm to prevent my escape. "Someone's got to keep an eye on the mighty All-Knowing seer. This quest's very important to all of us."

Saints have mercy! The thought of Ubaldo breathing down my neck while I was dealing with turning this fortune into reality was more than I could bear. I jerked my arm, but Ubaldo's fingers dug into my flesh.

Prince Leonato frowned. His leaf-green eyes flicked once between Ubaldo and me. "That won't be necessary, Master Ubaldo. No doubt the prophetess can take care of herself. My mother decreed only that the prophetess join in the quest. You will remain here, to await our return." With that, Leonato reached for Franca's rope himself, pulling the donkey forward. Ubaldo released me and jumped back, narrowly avoiding being stepped on by a heavy donkey hoof.

"But—" Ubaldo began.

Captain Ribisi cut him off. "Master Ubaldo, my men will see that you and your company have all that you require."

The two guards had Ubaldo halfway across the stable yard before he could speak another word. I patted Franca's neck, and she gobbled up the carrot that Snowdrop had spurned. I was so relieved to have Ubaldo gone that I did not realize for several long moments what had happened. The prince had spoken those words clearly. *Without falter.* I reviewed his last statement with furious consideration. A plan had begun to dawn on me.

Leonato himself didn't seem to have realized it. He still frowned after Ubaldo. "Are you really that man's s-s-servant?" he asked.

"No," I said. "Father and I are freeborn. We had to . . . that is, there was no other choice, and we had to travel with Ubaldo and his company."

"S-s-so you're glad that he's not coming with us?"

"More than glad," I said, speaking absolute truth for the first time in a long while. "Thank you, Your Highness."

"Good." Prince Leonato smiled, and I forgot to look away. Curse me to the seven Hells, I thought. I needn't fear Ubaldo, perhaps, but this was a worse danger. My belly had no business flopping over like that just because a handsome prince smiled at me. I had to find Leonato a wife, not fall in love with him myself.

THE NEXT DAY dawned gray and drizzly and the only pleasure I could take in it was that I hadn't prophesied fair weather for our departure. Nevertheless, the plaza was crowded with onlookers. If they did not cheer and huzzah for the prince, well, I suppose it was to be expected. They had seen this all end in failure many times before. But not today. I gritted my teeth and felt for the scroll of parchment tucked under my glittering, tattered robes. Not today.

I sat astride Franca, in the center of a crowd of guards. I could see Prince Leonato ahead of me, high atop the tower of horseflesh that was Snowdrop. The gelding had cleaned up rather nicely, in my opinion. He gleamed as white as snow, just as prophesied. That had not improved his temper, as I discovered when I tried to offer him another carrot that morning. I wondered how the stablehands had managed to wind those red ribbons through his mane and tail without being bitten.

Prince Leonato's cheeks burned as brilliantly as the ribbons, and his hands, gripping the reins, showed white at the knuckles. I hadn't found the opportunity to tell him about the scroll tucked beneath my robes. I hadn't even finished it until the morning bells of the cathedral launched the sleepy pigeons from the ledge outside my window. Nudging Franca's sides, I tried to ride close enough to speak to the prince. Just then a stir swept through the crowd. The stout guards between me and Prince Leonato paid me no heed as they turned to observe the cluster of figures that had emerged from the main palace doors.

The queen, garbed in her regal best and with a fixed smile on her lips, stood in the forefront. I spied my father as well: a small gray-haired figure, waving energetically and bobbing up on the tips of his toes to see me past the array of guards. Father seemed to be the only one truly enthusiastic about the morning's events.

"Jacopo, the prophecy," ordered the queen.

The same fat clerk stepped forth and read from a scroll of parchment. "Herein are recorded the exact words of the prophecy of the seer Fortunata, foretelling the quest of Prince Leonato, and how he shall fulfill the Edicts."

The queen beckoned to her son. "As the Edicts demand: *The Prince shall proclaim the Prophecy to the people, and its Truth shall ring from his lips without falter.* Come, my son, and fulfill your destiny."

Prince Leonato rode forward, with the look of a soldier heading into a battle he knew he couldn't win. Jacopo held out the scroll. The two guards in my path remained oblivious to Franca snorting down the backs of their necks. I fought the urge to let her trample them. I had to reach the prince before he tried to read that scroll. Slipping down from Franca, I pushed my way forward.

The tips of Prince Leonato's fingers had just brushed one end of the scroll in Jacopo's hand when I called out, "Wait!"

Every eye in the square turned upon me. My mouth felt dry as dead leaves, and the twisting in my belly made me glad I had not had the appetite for breakfast.

"Yes, Prophetess?" asked the queen, finally.

I cleared my throat and thought of Allessandra, how confident she seemed, how certain that the fortunes she spun were true. "I have had a vision," I began. A murmur stirred the crowd, heartening me slightly. "The prince will proclaim the prophecy, as the Edicts demand. Its truth will ring from his lips without falter. But *not* the words as I first spoke them, for I am but a humble seer. No, the True King must have a proclamation fit for royal blood. The Saints have granted me this magical scroll." I held aloft the parchment I had slaved over all night, to a flood of aahs and oohs from the crowd. Good, I thought. This just might work. "This magical scroll contains the truth of the prophecy, in words fit for a king."

Before anyone could object, I strode forward and slid my scroll into Prince Leonato's hands. "Go on," I said. "You can do it. It's your destiny." If only Leonato would believe me.

I clamped my lips tight then, for fear someone would catch me silently mouthing my prayers to the Saints. A hush fell over the crowd, expectant and eager. I risked a glance at the queen. She no longer stood with stiff reserve, but bent forward, hands clasped, eyes on her son. Yes, they all wanted to believe that this time it would work. Well, except for Captain Ribisi, who sat as gray and glum as a tombstone atop his own mount.

Prince Leonato unfurled the parchment with

trembling fingers. I gave him what I hoped was an encouraging smile, though my lips felt like old plaster, ready to crumble at the slightest touch. He scanned the words, took a deep breath, and opened his mouth.

"'I go forth now to rescue my future bride from Dire Peril and return with her in triumph to Doma, where we will be wed. I venture forth upon my proud mount, with his coat as white as winter's might. . . .'"

A crackle of excitement sped through the throng of onlookers. Even Prince Leonato paused for a moment. Then he went on, talking about the "royal footgear that will fit only a true princess" and the "mighty city that floats upon the river Balta" and stumbling over not a single syllable. Those had been the trickiest bits: replacing the references to Sirenza and shoes with words that didn't begin with the letter *S*.

"'Though I may face great danger, and terrible trials, yet my courage and honor will guide me true, and I will return to Doma with the Royal Maiden who will be my bride. That is the wisdom of the All-Knowing Eye,'" finished the prince.

The crash of cheers and applause seemed to shake the very cobbles of the square. My legs trembled as though a gust of wind might topple me over. I bowed my head. Saints be praised. It had worked.

A light touch brushed my shoulder. I looked up into Prince Leonato's eyes. "Thank you, Prophetess. I—"

The queen's voice rang out, interrupting whatever more the prince had been about to say. "People of Doma, you have heard the prophecy proclaimed by your prince. All that was foretold by the prophetess has been stated without falter, if not in the exact words as the original. My son, you have proven your worth to set out upon this quest." This pronouncement sent the crowds into another swell of applause and huzzahs.

"But, but, it wasn't the same words," sputtered Jacopo, waving the original scroll. Thankfully, his protests were lost in the clamor. The people of Doma embraced their prince's victory.

Prince Leonato wheeled Snowdrop around to salute them. If he felt any sorrow or fear at the prospect of leaving home, it was not evident in his face. His eyes shone with delight, and his cheeks were flushed with happiness, not shame. His golden hair clustered in rings at the nape of his neck and behind his ears. I had been hoping he might look less beautiful after I had gotten used to him, but it was not so. Even on this chill, gray day, he glowed like a small star, smiling over his people, loving them and loved by them.

The queen spoke again. "Prince Leonato, go now with the blessings of your people. Fulfill your fortune and return to us with your princess, that the Edicts may be satisfied. Take this slipper, which once bedecked the foot of Queen Rosetta herself, that you may know its twin."

At this, Princess Donata stepped forth. She held a silken pillow before her, upon which lay a single golden slipper. If I had not overheard her conversation yesterday, I would have thought her as delighted as the rest of the crowd. She smiled benevolently, though her lips twitched at the sight of Snowdrop, in irritation or amusement I could not tell.

The princess glided down the stairs to offer the pillow to Prince Leonato. He took the slipper reverently, then held it aloft and looked out over the people. "People of Doma," he called, "I go forth to fulfill the Edicts. You have my pledge that I will rule well and justly, and Doma will flourish once more."

A great huzzah rose from the crowds, and cheers of "Prince Leonato!" A number of the celebrants tossed their ribbons up into the air, showering us with coils of colored silk. Trumpeters arrayed along one side of the plaza began to play a triumphant march. This was it, the departure. The scarlet guards rode ahead, clearing the way from the plaza. Prince Leonato bowed his head to his mother, then turned Snowdrop from the palace. I pressed my heels against Franca's flanks, and we followed near the back of the procession. I turned to catch one last glimpse of Father, waving after me. I blinked against the tears that threatened. It would not do for the mighty prophetess to weep during the triumphal procession.

I had seen no sign of Ubaldo since the previous

afternoon, but when we neared the walls I caught sight of a familiar spotted horse ahead. I thought for a dreadful moment that he was going to join us, despite the prince's command. But as we drew near, I saw that the horseman was Coso. Ubaldo stood beside him and was handing the other man a long leather tube, of the sort used to hold scrolls. Coso nodded. Then Ubaldo slapped the horse, sending Coso off down the street toward the main gate.

I thought perhaps Ubaldo was sending Coso along with us, but as our procession passed from the city, I saw the spotted horse heading off down the western road, the way we ourselves had first come. My prophecy had said we would find the weapon to defeat the witch in a village three days to the east. What message did Coso bring west? What was Ubaldo up to? If I was in truth a seer, I might have known. But I had no way to find out.

I could not afford to worry about that, however. I had a fortune to make come true, and it would take all my wits to do it. Somewhere to the east, three days from here, was a village (I hoped), and somewhere in that village I would have to find a weapon that could slay a witch that didn't exist. I had a lot to think about.

CHAPTER

7

THE SUN HUNG LOW and red behind us on the third day, and I was beginning to get nervous. A grassy meadow rolled out before us, bounded north and south by darker forest. No candle or hearthfire twinkled within those empty slopes. We had passed the last farmer's house at noon. I'd been tempted to stop there, but I did not think even the prince, who *wanted* to believe, could be convinced that such a hovel might be considered a village. Other than that, we had seen no travelers.

We had spent the previous two nights at the mercy of what hospitality we could find. Perhaps hospitality wasn't the right word, as we were still within the demesne of Doma, and the people were obligated by fealty to serve their prince. But they seemed happy enough to offer Prince Leonato every comfort their simple homes could afford. We had left our escort behind as we passed out of sight of Doma, so it was only the prince, Captain Ribisi, and I who needed lodging. The captain slept rolled in his cloak, close by the prince. I found a soft nest in whatever hayloft was at hand.

"We must be almost there," Prince Leonato said, gazing toward the last curve of gold on the horizon. "The s-s-s— Curse it!" He slapped his thigh in frustration. "The s-s-s—"

"The sun's nearly set?" I prompted.

He groaned. "Why hasn't the magic lasted, Prophetess?" I quailed beneath his entreating gaze. Because it wasn't magic, I wanted to say.

He sighed. "I know, I know, it was only in the s-s-s-scroll. If only I could read from a magic s-s—parchment all the time, I'd be a proper prince."

"You seem a proper prince to me already, Your Highness."

He smiled without enthusiasm. "Not yet. But at least your prophecy gives me a hope of becoming one."

His high regard should have given me a thrill of excitement, but instead it shriveled me like a cold winter wind. Stop this, I told myself. It's no use feeling guilty. Remember, Father's life is at stake.

"I'll be glad to reach this village," said Prince Leonato. "I hope they have a proper inn. It was kind of that sh-sh-shepherd to give me his own pallet last night, but it was cursed uncomfortable."

Prince Leonato might doubt himself, but his zeal for my prophecy ran strong as a river in spring. "I'll go ahead; it's probably just over the next hill." He jogged Snowdrop's white flanks, and the large horse set off up the road at a pace remarkable in such an old beast.

I plodded onward, aware that Captain Ribisi was staring fixedly at me from atop his own brown mare. "What do you think he'll find?" Ribisi asked.

"The village, of course. As my fortune told."

"I don't believe in fortunes and prophecies."

"My prophecy got us this far. You yourself told me the others never even made it out of the city gates."

Captain Ribisi grunted. "I believe in what luck a person makes for himself. Or herself." He shot me a suspicious look.

My heart quailed. He had suspected from the start that I was a fake. But I couldn't show him my fear. "The prince believes in my fortune," I said. "Aren't you happy he made that proclamation without faltering?"

"Prince Leonato wants to be a hero. He's the mettle for it too. But he doesn't need some sham fortune to do it. Magic." He spat on the ground between us. "I gave up on that long ago."

"You did believe once, though," I extrapolated. "Something happened."

"It's no concern of yours," he said, staring furiously ahead. "Where's the prince got to now? Foolishness, fortunes, and prophecy. Bah."

"The fortune will come true," I said. I nudged Franca's sides, hoping to achieve a pace faster than her current plodding gait. Sweat slicked my palms. Try as I might, I couldn't make a village appear out of thin air. Then I heard shouting ahead.

Prince Leonato appeared over the crest of the hill, waving energetically. "The village, I've found it. Just as you s-s-said!"

Relief washed over me. I raised my chin and looked sideways at Ribisi. "See?"

MY SPIRITS ROSE as we approached the village. It was large; I could even make out the spire of a church against the darkening sky. Though less than a quarter of the size of Doma, it had a thick sturdy wall encircling the cluster of houses and buildings. Oddly, there were no buildings outside this wall, though we passed rich fields of barley and rye. Where did the farmers of those fields dwell?

The heavy wooden gates were already closed. In the last glimmer of sunlight, I made out a device carved over the gates. It looked like a sword plunged into a stone. That was promising. As we approached, a small square of wood midway up the door was pushed open, revealing a pair of suspicious eyes. "Travelers?" the man said.

The eyes flicked over Prince Leonato and Captain Ribisi, widening at the sight of the swords strapped to both their horses. "Warriors, at that. What business brings you to Saint Federica's Rest?"

In the face of proclaiming himself to a stranger, Prince Leonato wilted visibly. The enthusiasm that had carried him thus far vanished. He gulped, then started to speak. "Good eve, s-s-s-sir. We are here to s-s-search—"

"What? What's that? Speak up, boy! I can't make out a word you're saying."

Prince Leonato snapped his mouth closed, shoulders sagging. Saints' shadows! That was enough of that. "Give praise to the Saints, good man, for they have graced your city," I proclaimed in my most stirring theatrical voice. "Here stands before you Prince Leonato, upon a grand and noble quest for the glory of all Doma!"

The eyes blinked. "Prince, are you? And on a quest? Well, then, of course you are welcome within." The window banged shut, and shortly the wooden door swung open, revealing a beefy man with a full head of wiry black hair.

Prince Leonato prodded Snowdrop to start through the gate, but the porter stepped forward, blocking the way. "Your pardon, Prince Leonato, but you'll need to be leaving those blades with me 'fore you enter. Our village lies under the protection of Saint Federica. No weapons within these walls. That's our law."

Saint Federica, I remembered belatedly, was called "the peaceful." One of the stained-glass windows of the Valenzian cathedral had shown her being struck by the sword of evil King Rudolpho. Federica had been so pure the king's blade shattered as it touched her. Saint Federica had ever after been the patron of peacemakers.

"No weapons?" Prince Leonato repeated. "But I've come here to find a weapon to s-s-smite the Witch of the Black Wood. There must be a s-s-sword within."

"Oh, aye, there's one, and only one. The blade of the blessed Saint herself. You see, this was where she had her epiphany. She was a swordmaiden, 'fore she became a Saint. She fought a great battle here, long ago, and when she saw all the blood staining the land, the blood of her friends and companions who'd died, she swore never to touch a weapon again. She struck her sword then and there into a boulder. In time our people built up this village here. And since that day, there's never been any weapon save that one here in Saint Federica's Rest." The porter puffed up with pride as he told his tale. "'Twas my own great-great-great-grandsire who set the corner-stone of our church. We built it up over the very boulder itself, so's the sword would be in the center of the hall for all to see."

"Then that must be the weapon we s-s-seek," said the prince, turning to me. "Prophetess?"

"Yes," I said. What else was there to say? If the sword

of Saint Federica was the only blade in this village, it would have to do.

"Saint Federica herself wills it so," I continued on. "Upon the morrow, you shall go to the church and take up her blade, with her blessing."

"Here, now," said the porter. "Prince or no, you can't just come in and take a holy relic."

"It is the will of the Saint," I said.

"And you know the will of the Saint?" said the porter. "A little bit of a serving girl?"

"You're s-s-speaking to the great prophetess Fortunata the All-Knowing," Prince Leonato said, "and if sh-she s-says it is the will of the S-s-saint, then it is." I felt a glow of pride at the prince's words, until I remembered it was bought with lies.

"You can say what you like," countered the porter, "but it will be for Father Giotto to decide. He's the priest here."

"We will seek him out in the morning, then," said Captain Ribisi. "For now, Your Highness, we'd best find a place to sleep. You will need your strength for the morrow."

Prince Leonato nodded. Leaving their weapons with the porter, the prince and Captain Ribisi continued on into the village. I followed after them, barely noticing the trim white houses with their thatched roofs, and the curious faces peeking out the lighted windows. If Prince

Leonato was to have his sword, if my fortune was to come true, somehow I needed to convince the people of Saint Federica's Rest that their patron wished it so. And if the porter was any example, that would be a difficult task indeed.

THE INNKEEPER GAVE Prince Leonato her best suite of rooms. I even had a small alcove of my own, off the main sitting room, complete with a straw pallet and a tiny window that looked out over the courtyard behind the inn. I retired there as soon as I could, ostensibly to sleep. In actual fact, I doubted I would get any rest. There was too much to do before morning.

I nibbled at the cheese dumplings a serving girl had brought up and sipped my watered wine. The prince and Captain Ribisi were talking in the other room. I tried to sneak past their open door, but the captain had the ears of a hound, and I had to pretend I was merely fetching a drink of water. Captain Ribisi watched me like a hawk as I filled my cup and returned to my room, and I knew there was little chance of my getting out unnoticed while he was awake.

I sat curled up on my pallet, trying not to fall asleep. Through my window I heard a girl singing softly, accompanied by the soft creak of rope and wood and the splash of water. A serving girl fetching water from a well. Then a scent of smoke, and some deeper voices rumbling good-naturedly. Someone out for an evening pipe. Then they too fell silent. At last quiet swept over the inn like a quilted coverlet, until all was dim and peaceful, but for the creakings of the shutters and the skitterings of the mice.

I waited another long while, then cautiously made my way out into the main sitting room. I peered through the door to Prince Leonato and Captain Ribisi's room, and saw no sign of movement. Breathing a sigh of relief, I started toward the door. A floorboard creaked under my foot. I heard a snorting intake of breath from somewhere in the sitting room and froze. I peered through the gloom. To my distress, Captain Ribisi was seated at the writing desk. In the dim silvery light of the moon, I saw that he was slumped forward, asleep, judging by the sounds he made. A sheet of parchment lay before him, the quill hanging from his limp fingers. A burned-out candle sat nearby; the scent of its smoke lingered in the air. What was he writing at this hour of the night?

I crept closer, trying to peer over his shoulder. I could make out only the very top lines of the letter. *My beloved, though your royal station remains far above my own, know that I remain your loyal servant in this matter as in all things. Prince Leonato continues to*—. His arm obscured the rest. My mind struggled to fill in the blanks. Was Captain Ribisi the secret paramour of Princess Donata? Was he sending her reports on the prince? I suppressed an urge to tweak the paper out from under his elbow. He would surely wake, and I had other more pressing business.

I stepped carefully to the door, avoiding the creaky board, and exited the room. Out in the street, I breathed deeply at last as I took a moment to get my bearings. I could see the spire of the church, sharp against the starry sky. The first thing I'd do would be to get a look at this fabled sword of Saint Federica.

A few lamps burned yet, casting flickering golden light from their windows out across the cobbled street. I crouched for a moment behind a bin of flour outside the baker's shop, smelling the rich, sweet scent of nut cakes, already in the oven for the morning's market. I kept to the shadows and moved with as much stealth as I could manage, though my threadbare white gown was not the best costume for skullduggery. My fortune-telling costume would have been more appropriate, but I had left that packed away with my things at the inn.

I evaded a particularly brilliant lantern, hung up from the lintel of one of the houses, and slipped around the corner to confront the church. It was not so grand as a true cathedral, but it was still larger than any of the other buildings in the village. Lights flared within, but that didn't surprise me. The sacred candles were kept burning throughout the night. There might even be a cleric on hand to tend to them, but he'd probably be asleep at this hour.

I entered the vestibule, then peered through the arched doorway into the worship hall. I could see no one. A smattering of flames danced among the bank of small candles arrayed at the front, before the icons of the Saints. From this distance I could not distinguish one icon from the next. There were so many Saints, and one looked much like the next, if you could not see the distinctive trappings. I could tell the large statue at the far right was Saint Bartolommeo the generous, with his great sack of toys and sweets rising like a hunch on his burly shoulder. And the woman with the vast carved wings must be Saint Angelica, who watched over children and kept them from harm. There were a dozen more, and in the very center, under the great roseate window, gleamed a glint of metal amid the gray and white of granite and marble. The blade of Saint Federica, just as the porter had described, plunged deep into a boulder. Above the rough bulk of the rock rose a hand span of glittering blade and graceful crossguard.

I was about to step forward into the hall when a noise stopped me short. I was not alone. A man sat in the front pew, sprawled against the carved wooden back. By the long purple robes and white mantle I knew it must be the priest himself, though his garments hung all askew and his gold sash was tossed haphazardly over a nearby pedestal holding jars of ceremonial oils.

The priest raised his hand, and the candlelight

glittered on what he held. A goblet. He raised it, as if toasting the statues of the Saints, then tossed back its contents. He staggered to his feet and lurched a few steps up to the other pedestal, which held the jar of sacred wine. With an unsteady hand, he sloshed a great quantity into his cup, then swallowed that down as well. He hiccuped, and poured out another measure.

I watched this spectacle in amazement. I suppose, given my own sinful activities, I wasn't in any position to judge the priest. But really! Drinking the sacred wine!

None of this helped my situation, however. At least, not as far as I could see. I chewed on my lower lip, considering my options. What was I to do? I had to persuade this priest to allow Prince Leonato to take the sword. Must I conjure forth a sign from the heavens? Call down the Saint herself to speak her will?

Hmmm. There was a thought. I had summoned up spirits before. How different would a Saint be? And this priest was wine-addled enough that he just might believe it. All I needed were a few supplies. I didn't have the white paint and gauzy robe; those were back in the blue wagon, in Doma. But I thought I could find something to suit, with a bit of pilfering about the village.

A short time later, I had what I needed. I scouted around the back of the church and found a convenient window partway up the rear wall, beside the larger roseate stained glass. A bit more rummaging, and I had procured a rickety ladder from the nearby stables. I wished there were a mirror, so I could check the effect of my costume, but I had to make do with the surface of the water in the watering trough.

A ghostly figure stared back at me. My white gown didn't trail in long gauzy folds like the spirit veil, but it would do well enough. The handful of flour I'd nipped out of the baker's barrel had turned my hair and skin pasty white. I did give off small puffs of powder with every move, but I rather thought they added to the impression of ethereality.

Teetering at the top of the ladder, I set the bright lantern from the house around the corner down on a narrow ledge below the window. That would backlight me nicely, with an aura suitable for a Saint. I could see the priest down in the hall below. He had moved on to taking mouthfuls directly from the wine bottle. I cleared my throat, and began.

"Priest of the Saints. . . ." I pitched my voice low, so that it filled the church with a sibilant echo.

The priest started. He turned this way and that, looking for the source of the words.

"I, Saint Federica, come now before you."

He saw me. Hastily, he pushed the bottle of wine back onto the pedestal, then retreated unsteadily, tripping over his purple robes. "Oh, Saint Federica, forgive me!" he wailed. "I did not mean to drink the sacred wine. Please don't punish me, oh, blessed lady!" He remained where he had fallen upon the stone floor, knocking his head against it in genuflection.

"You have trespassed most grievously, priest," I said, allowing a more ominous edge into my voice. No sense in wasting the fellow's fear. A little terror of celestial retribution would make him much easier to manipulate. "You have taken what is holy and used it to satisfy your own impure vices. For such acts, you surely deserve punishment."

"Please, I beg you, blessed one. I meant no harm. I'm a weak man. But I'll make up for it, I promise you."

Good. Just where I wanted him. "Will you do what you must to atone for these ills, priest? Will you be the hand of the Saints on earth and do our righteous will?"

"Oh, yes, Saint Federica, I swear it on your own sweet name!"

"Then fear not, priest. Your transgressions shall be overlooked, for now. I have come with a far greater purpose. I have a task for you, my faithful servant."

"Anything, anything, blessed one." He looked up, eyes wide, hands clasped.

"I bring a message to you and all who dwell within this village. You must see that it is heard. A great warrior has come into my demesne. A holy warrior, with noble purpose. He goes forth to vanquish great evil. He has come here by my will, to take up my blade and bear it hence from the village." I swept one hand out to point at the sword, sending a drift of flour misting down over the icons below.

"Your sword, Saint Federica? But it has been here beyond recollection!"

"Do not question my will!"

He quailed under my fierce words and genuflected again. "No, of course not, blessed one."

"Too long has this last remnant of war and death remained within these walls. The sword shall be drawn from the stone by the holy warrior and taken from here. Then, a new icon shall be carved in my honor, an icon of peace alone. And my blessings upon this village shall be many.

"Now, cast down your sinful brow, and do penance of a hundred prayers in my name. Then you shall go and take your rest in peace. And in the morning, ready yourself for the coming of the warrior."

"Yes, Saint Federica, yes. Thank you, thank you for your blessings!" He cast himself down again, and I heard the muttered singsong of his prayers. As soon as I was sure he was intent upon this task, I began to lower myself down the ladder.

One hundred prayers gave me plenty of time to replace the ladder and the lamp, though it would take a bit more effort to get the flour off my skin and out of my hair. I shook clouds of powder from my hair as I stood in the dark stable doorway, watching the front of the church. It was not long before I saw the priest depart. After he had stumbled away down the street, I entered the church once more. I had one more thing to check, and then I could retire to my own bed in peace.

I strode to the front of the hall, stepping carefully around the puddles of sacred wine that tracked the floor. I seized the hilt of Saint Federica's sword and gave it a gentle tug. Several inches of silver blade pulled up from the rough stone, as easily as from a scabbard. Good. Prince Leonato should have no problem fulfilling this part of my fortune.

A rustling sound sent my heart thumping. Had the priest returned? I scanned the dim hall, and saw nothing. It was probably mice. My work here was done, and I was eager to return to the inn.

I made my way back quickly, but paused at the threshold of the inn, catching sight of myself in the diamond panes of the small window beside the front door. I was still a sight, covered in flour, my long hair loose and unbraided. I would have to do something about that before retiring. I could imagine what Captain Ribisi would think if he saw me in this state in the morning. He was clever as a cat, that man.

I slipped around behind the inn, through a side gate that led to the courtyard I had glimpsed from the window of my room. It was a charming place, separated from the stables and other nearby buildings by a thick hedge. I followed a path of pale stepping stones between clumps of plants and taller bushes. Potherbs for the cook, judging by the spicy scents that filled the air. At the end of the path I found the well I had heard the serving girl drawing water from earlier. The moon had fled the sky, but the night was bright with stars. By their glimmer, I spied a wide stone basin beside the well. I heaved up a half-filled bucket from the well, wincing at each creak of the rope. No lights flared in the windows above. I sloshed the water into the basin and proceeded with my ablutions.

The clink of the gate latch told me someone had entered the courtyard. I lifted my head from the basin in alarm. I was clad only in my chemise, and my limbs streamed rivulets of dusty water. My gown lay across a clump of rosemary, where I had tossed it after shaking it free of flour.

"Is s-s-someone there?" a young man's voice called softly. My heart did a skip-beat. What was Prince Leonato doing roaming about in the middle of the night?

There was no way out. The thick hedge bounded the yard on all sides. I would have to make the best of the situation. "It's just me, Fortunata," I answered. I snatched up my dress, but had only time to clutch it to myself before the prince reached the well. "Your Highness," I said, attempting a curtsy. My loose, wet (but flour-free) hair slithered forward over my shoulders. I pushed it back with one hand, hoping I had gotten the last bits of flour off my face and arms.

"Oh! I'm s-s-s-s—" Even in the dim light of the stars I could see a flush stain his cheeks. My own face felt as if it must be burning just as brightly. He gave up trying to get the word out and turned abruptly to face a pear tree in the corner of the garden.

I threw on my gown, lacing the bodice haphazardly. "Is that part of having the S-s-sight?" he said after a moment. "Bathing by s-s-starlight?" He was looking up at the sky. I could see the strong line of his brow, under its cluster of golden curls. I twisted my own hair into a rough knot at the nape of my neck, making myself at least somewhat presentable.

"Something like that," I said, grinning despite myself. "You can turn around."

"You look different," Prince Leonato said.

"I'm wearing my dress now, Your Highness."

"No, I mean different from before." He looked at me intently. My face, if possible, felt even hotter. "It's the robes and the headdress," he said at last. "I didn't realize you were s-s-so young."

"I'm nearly eighteen," I protested. "And besides, you can't be much older than that yourself."

He blinked. Belatedly, I realized one wasn't supposed to contradict princes.

"Nineteen in s-s-six months," he said. "That's why Mother's s-s-so worried. The Edicts must be fulfilled before then. On my S-s-saint's Day, if I haven't rescued a princess and been betrothed, the crown will go to my aunt."

"Would that be so bad?" I asked. "You said yourself you know how hard it is to be king."

"Yes, well. . . ." He hesitated. "It's not proper to s-s-speak ill of your own relations. But—"

"Princess Donata would not make a good queen?"

He did not answer at first, but stood staring into the shadows. "When I was a little boy, I used to s-s-sneak down to the kitchens, to visit the cook. He was a jolly old fellow, reminded me of S-s-saint Bartolommeo. He never laughed at my s-s-s—at the way I talk." Leonato lowered his eyes to the nearest flowerbed, running his fingers absently through the leaves. A breath of rosemary filled the air. "He always had a biscuit or a few candied fruits for me. My aunt caught me with some of his s-s-sweets one day, leaving s-s-sticky fingerprints on the chairs. She ordered the cook beaten. Father was away, fighting s-s-some other king, and Mother was ill. I tried to help, I tried to order the guards to s-s-s—"

Each halting syllable seemed to hit the prince like a blow as he struggled to get the word out. At last he slapped one hand against his thigh, giving a sort of strangled groan. I feared to speak, not knowing if it would make him feel even worse. I knew what he was trying to say, and it was horrible.

After a long moment in which I stared at the stars and Prince Leonato took deep breaths of herb-scented air, he finally spoke again.

"My aunt told me that if I couldn't even control myself to give a s-s-simple order like that, I didn't have the right to give them."

"The cook?" I asked.

"S-s-sent away. I never s-s-saw him again, though I looked. He could barely crawl." Prince Leonato knelt beside a large yarrow plant; he plucked a stalk tipped with a heavy white flower head. "My aunt told me it was my fault Cook had been beaten, because I asked him for s-s-sweets I wasn't s-s-supposed to have. She told me I was a greedy child who wanted everything he could get, and that I needed to learn that others would s-s-suffer for it." He shook his head abruptly. I could not see his face, but his voice was tight. He cleared his throat. "What is this plant?" he asked, raising the flower.

"Yarrow. It's said to protect against evil." Allessandra had taught me something of herbcraft, and yarrow was common enough. "You've never seen it?"

"No, not in the gardens, nor anywhere in Doma." He crushed the pale flowerets between his fingers, bending his head over the handful and sniffing.

I had been afraid of Princess Donata before this,

dismayed at her promise to see my fortune fail. Now I hated her, for bringing any sorrow into Leonato's life. He wanted to do good. He wanted to *be* good, and she had made him doubt that. I'd have liked to tear her throat out. But she was not here. Just Leonato, and his misery. And me, desperately wishing I could bring back his smile.

"It wasn't your fault," I said. I extended my hand, to do what I didn't know. Pat him on the shoulder? I had forgotten he was a prince by then. He turned around to face me, and I snatched my hand back. "I'm sure the cook is well enough now, and that he doesn't blame you," I said.

"Truly?" Leonato's face brightened. "You s-s-see him, Prophetess?"

I writhed inwardly. I could comfort him, but only with lies.

"It must be amazing," he went on, "to have s-s-such powers. You always know what lies ahead; you don't have to worry if you'll s-s-succeed, or if you'll be good enough. All I can think about is failing. I've failed s-s-so many times. This is my last chance." He paced around the side of the well, scuffing his boots against the stones. A climbing rose twined up the well-house, its white blossoms bright even in the gloom. The prince twisted one of the thorny vines absently, as he stared down into the dark waters.

I had never more wanted to be able to speak the truth. To be able to tell the prince how fear crouched in my own chest like a lump of iron. How I had dreamed last night of my father kneeling at the headsman's block, the great silver ax sweeping down toward his neck because I had failed. If we could only share our fears, perhaps they would not seem so dark. If only I could slip my hand into his, lead him forward to confront our terrors together. "You will succeed," I said at last.

He grimaced into the well. "It's funny, isn't it? I have the words of a True S-s-seer to believe in. But here I am, rambling around in the middle of the night fighting off fears that I might not be good enough. Even though I know the s-s-sword is here, and that you have s-s-seen me taking it." Saints smile on him, where had he gotten such eyes? I felt sure he must see through me, all the petty thoughts and lies I'd told. And was still telling. I couldn't bear to be false with him.

The words tried to force their way through my lips, admitting my deception, revealing that this whole prophecy was a farce. But I pushed them back ruthlessly. I had to think of Father. "I have foreseen it. Don't fear, Your Highness. You will succeed."

"Thank you, Prophetess," he said after a moment. He held out the single white rose he'd broken off.

"It's Fortunata, Your Highness. You needn't give me titles," I said. Especially when I didn't deserve them. He did not lower the rose, so I took it at last, wincing as the thorns pricked my fingers. It was beautiful, though the strong scent made me light-headed. I must be imagining the look in his eyes; it was the reflection of the starlight, nothing more. Yet how desperately I wished it *were* more, that I had brought that light and sparkle to him.

He grinned. "I'll s-s-stop using your title, if you'll do the s-s-same with mine. Leonato is fine." I was sure the solid flagstones beneath my feet had turned to moonbeams, or clouds, or some other gorgeous, insubstantial substance. My heart beat like it held a thousand butterflies.

"Won't that be improper?" I asked, trying to escape my bewilderment in humor.

"Maybe if I were king," he said. "But I'm not, yet."

The words yanked me back down toward solid reality. I clutched the rose, but I couldn't hold fast to those glorious dreams. It was madness. I must make him king, I told myself. And to do so, I needed to find him a princess in dire peril. I couldn't very well be making eyes at him in a dark garden. I struggled to speak the words that would send him away.

"It's very late, Your Highness," I said. "And you have much to do on the morrow. You should try to sleep."

He nodded. "Good night, Fortunata."

"Good night," I said, as the gate creaked shut and his golden head was lost in the gloom. "Leonato." I realized

I was holding the white rose so tightly a thorn had pierced my palm. An echoing pain throbbed in my breast, where I had let an impossible dream slip in. In that brief span, standing together in the garden, something had spun out of the fragrant air between us. It might not stand the light of day, but I treasured it. I took the bloom with me when I returned to my small chamber. It was late, but for what little of the night that remained, I dreamed of roses and green eyes.

THE NEXT MORNING I dressed myself in the glittering fortune-telling costume. I didn't think the priest would recognize me, but better to take no chances. My hair was still damp; I rebraided it and tucked the coils under my starry headdress.

Unfortunately, though my nighttime scrubbing had removed all traces of my saintly impersonation, they had also given me an undesired gift. My head ached, and my throat felt like I'd swallowed coarse salt. My nose was stuffed up, giving me a very un-prophetess-like sniffle. I had just brewed a pot of lemon tea in the hopes of clearing my head when we were summoned to the church.

My ruse had worked even better than I had hoped. By the time we reached the shadow of the church spire, the priest had already gathered up most of the villagers to see the holy warrior who had come with the blessing of Saint Federica herself. I heard the story a dozen times before we even reached the building. In some versions, Saint Federica had flown in through the windows and set every candle in the hall alight. In others, she had sprung forth from the sword itself. But in all, she had brought a command that must be obeyed. "And she'll shower blessings upon us," said one woman. "Think of that. What sort of blessings, do you suppose?"

Anything good that happened in the next dozen years, I thought, would be cast up as a blessing of Saint Federica. I was pleased. Everything was working out as I planned. Except this silly cold. I sipped at my mug of lemon tea, which I had brought with me. Mother had always warned me about sleeping with a head of wet hair.

The church was crammed with people, and we had to pass up the steps between a press of onlookers. I slipped to the side as we entered the hall, finding a spot beside one of the great stone columns, where I could sip my tea quietly and watch the priest and Leonato perform their parts for the crowds.

Leonato looked just as a prince on a grand quest ought to look. His doublet was of dark golden velvet, slashed at the sleeves to show the undershirt of wheat-colored silk. His hose were dusky amber, a color like fine honey. He carried himself proudly, with no hint of the anxiety I had seen last night. As he strode down the hall, he gave me a brief, glowing smile that warmed me more than the hot tea.

Captain Ribisi was dressed in his finest as well, but the bright scarlet and white made his grizzled hair dull and his scarred face more fierce. Beside him, Leonato appeared even more the image of Saint Marco. The clamoring crowds quieted as Leonato approached the sword. The priest bowed, spreading his hands wide in a welcoming gesture. His white hood hung straight, though I could just make out wine stains down the front of his purple robes.

"Prince of Doma, you are welcome to the sacred church of Saint Federica. Your coming is truly a blessing, heralded in this very chamber by the spirit of the Saint herself." The priest turned to face the crowded pews. "People of Saint Federica's Rest. Many of you have already heard of the miraculous happenings that transpired last evening. As I lay prostrate in this very church, in earnest prayer to the Saints, I was visited by a stunning apparition."

I snorted into my tea at this, but fortunately the oohs and ahhs of the crowd covered the noise. He went on, "The blessed Saint herself appeared to me and spoke of the coming of this holy warrior, who would take up her blade and wield it in the cause of goodness and righteousness. She hovered there"—he pointed up to the roseate window—"a vision of light and purity. Her voice was like the bells that ring in the Hall of Saints." The priest lifted his feverish eyes to the heavens, outstretched hands trembling. "And now the prophesied warrior has come, and it is the hour for the sword of Saint Federica to be claimed for its new task."

The priest stepped aside, waving Leonato forward to the sword. It stood gleaming just as I had seen it last night, struck into the great boulder. Leonato's back was turned to me, but I saw his shoulders rise and fall, as if he had taken a deep breath. Then he stepped forward, set his hand on the hilt, and pulled.

It did not move. I could see Leonato straining mightily, but the sword held fast within the stone. There was barely time to think. I knew I had to act immediately, lest my whole deception fall down and bury us all. The people clustered around me had already started murmuring in confusion. It would soon turn to suspicion, then anger.

"Impurity! Sin!" I called out, my voice froggy but still loud enough to cut through the muttering. "Someone within these walls has brought the taint of sin into the presence of the blessed Saint Federica. We must make prayers and offerings to the Saint, to appease her wrath!" I pushed my way forward toward the front of the hall. As I passed, villagers bent their heads, chanting prayers. The priest flushed nearly as dark as his own robes and chafed his hands against each other. I could guess the thoughts behind that guilt-stricken face.

"Fortunata, what's going on?" Leonato whispered as I stepped up beside him to look at the sword.

I saw the true problem immediately. The yellowish residue around the juncture of blade and stone told me what had happened. Someone had poured wax into the crevice, and it had hardened, holding the sword fast within the stone.

"We must all send up prayers to the Saint, to cleanse this church of the taint within," I called out. I muttered a prayer of my own, that Saint Federica would take pity on me, and show me a way to get out of this mess. My father's life was on the line, after all. And she was patron of peace. All I wanted was peace.

The priest threw himself down before the altar at that, nearly knocking over the jar of holy oil. He began rattling off prayers in a blur of barely recognizable words. Leonato knelt on my other side, clasping his hands, closing his eyes, and taking up his own prayers.

I realized I was still holding my mug of tea, and inspiration struck. "We must make offerings to the blessed Saint," I said. I snatched the jar of sacred oil from the pedestal, and cast it down over the stone. In the same motion, I dumped my steaming tea onto the crevice. I hoped it would be hot enough.

"Now," I said, "we have paid homage to Saint Federica, and granted unto her the sacred oils. Prince Leonato, take up the holy blade."

He rose, serene and sure, seeming to glow as if he truly were the holy warrior I had named him. Stepping forward, he seized the blade and drew it from the stone in one smooth motion. The hot lemon tea and perfumed oil cast up billows of sweet scent. Leonato turned to face the crowds, a triumphant smile on his lips.

"May holy Federica be praised," he cried. "Blessings upon you, priest, and all the people of this fair village. With this holy blade, I will go forth and undertake my next quest: to vanquish the evil Witch of the Black Wood!"

I wondered if there might really have been some Saintly influence at work just then, or if Leonato was just lucky to have avoided any troublesome *S* words in that speech. The cheers of the crowd filled the church, as every soul within gave voice to their joy for this blessing of the Saints. No, not every soul, I realized. Captain Ribisi stood to the side of the altar, beside the statue of Saint Bartolommeo. Unlike that jolly Saint, Ribisi was glowering. Not at the jostling crowds that now streamed from the pews, eager to share the news of the day with those outside. Not at the priest, who was fawning over Prince Leonato. No, the captain's scowl was fixed on me.

I had a good idea why. Someone had tried to thwart my fortune. Princess Donata had said herself she would have someone ready to interfere. Could that person be the prince's own loyal guard?

CHAPTER

8

P RINCE LEONATO determined that he would remain
at the church to make his prayers to the Saints for
their blessing. Captain Ribisi stayed close by, of course.
I, on the other hand, wanted to get as far away from
that church as possible. I had been too busy to panic
before this, but now the fears flooded back, turning
my legs weak as water. I had come perilously close to
failure.

Captain Ribisi was working against me—I was sure
of it. The sword had been tampered with. I remembered
the noises I had heard while I stood there with my hand
upon the hilt last night. Had Captain Ribisi been out
there? Watching me, waiting for me to leave? Now that
his first attempt to thwart my fortune had failed, what
would he do?

My belly was rumbling, and I needed a place to sit and think. I returned to the inn to cozy myself away in a corner with a platter of mushroom dumplings and a cup of watered wine. As I ate, my thoughts settled a bit. Perhaps I was jumping to conclusions about Captain Ribisi. He'd been sleeping in the sitting room last night when I returned, in the same position at the writing desk as earlier. But there had been plenty of time for him to slip back in while I was washing at the well. And there had been that letter. A report to his mistress, Princess Donata?

I pulled my thoughts back to the fortune itself. After all, if I couldn't produce the next bit of it, there would not be anything for my mysterious opponent to thwart. So. The next task was to find the witch. The Black Wood lay to the north. Perhaps, with luck, I could find some old herb-woman to fill the role. Though I didn't relish the idea of seeing an innocent old granny cut down by Leonato in his enthusiasm. And there was still the shoe to worry about.

I glanced about the inn, wondering if there was a shoemaker in Saint Federica's Rest. The room was crowded, more so than it had been when we first arrived. I soon understood why.

"Here in this very inn," one of the men was saying, jabbing his pipe up at the ceiling, "on a quest, drawn the holy blade of Saint Federica herself."

"Golden hair and green eyes, and handsome as Saint

Marco himself," tittered a red-haired serving maid to a cluster of other women. "Looking for a bride, so I've heard. A princess under a spell, so's she doesn't even know she's a princess. But he's to wake her with a kiss."

I stuffed a dumpling into my mouth to keep from laughing at that. No one would believe such twaddle.

"I heard it was a pair of magic slippers," said one of the women.

"No, the princess is imprisoned by an ogre, and the prince must slay it."

"He has a magic horse, I heard. It speaks to him and flies swifter than an eagle."

They fell into an argument, and I turned my ears to other conversations. Everyone was talking of Prince Leonato and the quest. More people crammed in through the doors every few moments, doubtless come from the spectacle at the church. The extravagant variations on my fortune being tossed about the commons were sometimes so far-fetched I had trouble even recognizing them.

"I hope he does kill that witch." A querulous voice rose from near the great hearth. An old man with a few wisps of white hair sat on a bench drawn close beside the flames. "She's been a nuisance since I was a boy. I remember when Queen Rosetta herself came to deal with the hag."

"There truly is a witch?" I asked in a loud voice that

drew several interested looks. Belatedly, I realized I was still dressed in my fortune-telling garb, though I had set aside the headdress.

"Oh, stop your silliness, Pasquale. That witch is just a story to frighten children," someone said.

"She's not just a story. I've seen her. She's out there, all right. Stealing children away to cook them in her stew."

"You're the prophetess, aren't you?" asked the red-headed serving maid. "The one who foresaw all this? Tell me, have you seen the face of the princess in your visions? What does she look like?"

"You mean, does she have carrot-red hair and a freckled nose?" asked one of the other women. "Don't get your hopes up, Teresa. You heard that the princess is in Sirenza."

Teresa wrinkled her nose and tossed back her red hair. "I've been to Sirenza."

"But the princess is in dire peril, isn't she, Prophet-ess?" the other woman asked.

"Yes, terrible danger." I was more interested in what Pasquale had said. "You've heard of the Witch of the Black Wood? Where . . . that is, my visions told me of a horrible hag in the dark woods. But it was a bit . . . unclear. If you know more of this witch, anything that might help the prince to defeat her and regain the, er, magic slipper, please tell me."

Everyone had some wisdom to offer. Unfortunately, most of the stories seemed to contradict one another, or else they were so wildly improbable that they must have been the product of fancy rather than fact. One old woman insisted she had seen the witch flying overhead on her demon horse, white as bone with flaming eyes. I sifted through the tales, gaining precious little that might be truth. But it was more than I'd started with.

A trail ran north into the Black Wood, peeling off from the main road at the stand of three oak trees. Those oldsters who could remember when Queen Rosetta had come to the region all agreed that she had taken that way into the wood. "Fair and noble she was," one man said. "Clad all in white, with those golden slippers, looking like the moon in the night seated on her black mare. Ah, such a beauty."

A number of farmers who had come from a village to the east insisted that the witch came to their village every Feast of Fools to sell charms at the great market. "Horrible old hag," insisted one. "Wartier than a toad, though not so green."

I tucked away all this information, halfheartedly nibbling on the nut cake that finished my meal. The best we could do, then, was to follow that same road. I knew that there was truth at the heart of any wild rumor. Somewhere up that road there was an old herb-woman who made frivolous little charms to cure baldness and remove freckles but had no more real magic than I. Whether she might truly have the queen's slipper, I didn't know. I had best look into finding a suitable shoe for Leonato to recover from the supposed witch. I stuck the nut cake into my pouch for later and left the inn in search of a shoemaker.

WE SET OUT the next day. The people of Saint Federica's Rest thronged the streets to send Leonato on his way, cheering and even casting flowers over our small procession. Leonato rode up beside me as we continued on through the cheery meadows and fields of barley. I became painfully conscious of how red my nose must be, although my sniffle seemed to be passing. He's a prince, I told myself, gripping the reins to stay focused, a prince looking for a princess. It doesn't matter if your nose is red. My heart, ignoring this sensible advice, proceeded to do flip-flops as Leonato leaned closer, looking me over with concern.

"Are you feeling better?" he asked.

"What?" Surprise made the word come out sharper than I intended.

"I thought you looked unwell yesterday. I was worried, when I s-saw you in the church."

Leonato was worried about me! The thought blew

over me like the sweetest warm summer breeze. I realized I should be saying something. "Thank you. I feel much better now."

"Are you s-sure you don't want to s-s-stay another night in the village, to rest?"

In that moment, all I wanted to do was to lose myself in his green gaze. But my senses had not departed entirely. I shook my head. "We need to find the other slipper." And the princess, I reminded myself. My throat tightened at the thought, sending me into a fit of coughing. I bowed forward over Franca's long ears, trying to recover.

"Here," said Leonato, holding out a small wooden box. "I thought you could use these. They're lemon candies, s-s-sweetened with honey. The apothecary said they would s-s-soothe a cough."

As I took it, his fingers brushed against mine, jolting me with a strange, tingling shiver. I nearly expected Franca to start, but she plodded on. "Thank you," I managed at last. He gave me one more glorious smile, then nudged Snowdrop ahead so he could speak with the captain.

I watched him go. Every tiny detail sparkled, like the gilt illuminations in one of the great books of the Saints: the curve of his lips when he smiled, the hope that flashed brightly in his eyes, the delight he took in the green fields and flowering meadows.

I popped one of the lozenges into my mouth. It soothed my throat, as promised, but it could not soothe my troubled thoughts. I told myself the prince was only being kind. As he'd been kind to every farmer, priest, or crafter we'd met on our journey. He wasn't courting me—that was ridiculous. Wasn't it? I was being foolish. I clamped down on the candy so forcefully it shattered, leaving me to suck on lemony splinters. Better to turn my mind to the problem at hand than to trouble over these flights of fancy.

I still had no suitable shoe. There was no shoemaker in all of Saint Federica's Rest. Their needs were served by a traveling crafter who was not due to visit again for another two months. I was so distracted by thoughts of how to produce a golden slipper I did not notice we had reached the three oaks until Franca halted abruptly and flicked back her ears at me. The two men had stopped ahead.

"It's as you foretold," Leonato said, beaming up at the trees. "Three oaks to mark the path to the Black Wood. Do you s-s-suppose the witch knows we're coming? Will sh-she call down her magics upon us when we enter?" His eyes were not wide and fearful, as one might expect upon entering the lair of a wicked witch. Instead, they shone bright with excitement. Leonato's success with the sword had invigorated him.

The energy had also, apparently, touched Snowdrop.

The old horse strained forward, stamping his great feet impatiently. Captain Ribisi took the lead. "I will go first, my prince, to make certain the way is safe."

Was he planning a trap, something to thwart my fortune? I kept a close eye on the man as we entered the woods.

The Black Wood was well named. Only a dim, misty light filtered down through the canopy of oak leaves, though it was nearly noon and the day was clear. There was very little undergrowth, so the thick gray boles of the trees stretched out like pillars in an endless hall. I felt small and meek. It was no comfort to be able to see into the depths of the forest, unobscured by bramble and brush; it seemed endless and grim, and before long, I lost all sense of direction. We had only the road to guide us, and that had quickly narrowed to a single mossy track. The noises of the wood seemed to echo, as if we were in some vast cavern. The patter of falling acorns, the scampering of some small creature, all were cast back to us, magnified into the sinister scuttlings of some far more terrible beast.

"Did you know your grandmother?" I asked Leonato, raising my voice to carry forward. "Did she ever speak of the witch?"

"Sh-she died when I was very young," he said, twisting in the saddle to look back at me. "My father told me the s-s-story. Grandmother came to the witch to ask for her blessing upon the lands—there was a drought, I think—but the witch was evil and refused. The witch s-s-started to put a s-s-spell on Grandmother. Grandmother escaped, but not before the witch caught one of her golden s-s-slippers. Grandmother didn't dare to return for it."

I was about to ask what sort of spell it had been, when Leonato abruptly reined back Snowdrop and reached for his sword. "What is it?" I asked.

He arced the blade to the left, near the bole of a tree close beside the trail. The sword sank into the bark with a thunk, followed by an angry stream of chittering. I caught the flash of a brushy gray tail retreating up into the boughs above.

"Just a squirrel, Your Highness," I said, brushing bits of splintered wood and bark off my sleeves and out of Franca's tufted mane.

He grimaced, tugging the blade loose. "This cursed place is getting on my nerves. I'm expecting to find the witch lurking around every turn. You must think I'm a fool," he added, glancing back. "Your S-s-sight would have warned if we were to be attacked."

"Not a fool, just very . . . alert," I said, smiling. "And I don't always foresee everything."

"What's going on back there?" Captain Ribisi had drawn his brown mare around. "Are you well, my prince?"

"Yes, Captain. I'm only s-s-seeing phantoms and mauling innocent trees."

Ribisi looked from the tree to Leonato's sword. "Well, it's good to see the legendary sword of prophecy didn't shatter on the first blow."

"Of course it wouldn't," said Leonato. "It's a holy s-s-sword."

"Hmmph," was all Ribisi said. "Come along, then. We'd better keep going if we're to find this supposed witch." He turned his mount back down the trail and set off.

"Are we going the right way?" Leonato asked me, after sheathing his sword.

"This is the only road," I said, falling back on truth.

"The witch must be nearby. This forest prickles my s-s-skin. I feel like it's watching us. Perhaps she's enchanted the trees to s-s-serve her." Snowdrop continued onward without prompting, still full of unwarranted energy. I, on the other hand, had to coax Franca forward, for she was growing increasingly balky.

Something whistled through the air before me. For a heartbeat I thought it was a bird, before I saw the quivering shaft sunk deep into the tree to my left. It *was* a trap. I had said myself this was the only road. Someone else knew our way and had lain in wait for us.

"An attack!" Leonato called. "It's the witch!"

"Bandits," Captain Ribisi said. "Take cover!" The

captain turned his mare to the right and charged off the trail.

Several more arrows whizzed through the air, one of them passing just over Franca's ears. The normally placid donkey snorted and reared back. I tumbled off, landing painfully against a tangle of roots.

"Fortunata!"

A whoosh of horsebreath blew over me. Rubbing my head, I looked up to see Leonato leaning down from the saddle with a worried expression. "Are you hurt? We have to help Captain Ribisi!"

I thought to myself that Captain Ribisi was probably perfectly safe. He might well have been the one who arranged this ambush. "Where is he?"

"Chasing them down. He'll need help. Here, you can ride with me." Leonato reached out to help me up, but pulled back abruptly, staring at something behind me. He brandished his sword with a flourish, calling, "Back, foul creatures! Back before the holy blade of Federica. The dark arts of your mistress will not avail you!"

There were three of them. For a long moment I was almost convinced they were creatures of the witch: trolls and goblins summoned up to do her bidding. But they were men. It was the layers of dirt, the ragged clothing, the gap-toothed snarling grins, and the murderous light in their eyes that made them appear as monsters.

One of them carried a long, wicked dagger, another

a sturdy ax. The third held a spear, its point glittering dangerously near to Leonato as he rode toward them. I looked around wildly for Captain Ribisi, but there was no sign of him. There was no sign of Franca either. She was probably out of the woods by now and making for a warm stable and a manger full of hay. "Get him, lads!" said the man with the dagger, leering at the prince. "He's the one."

My stomach turned over. Even the holy blade of Saint Federica would not help us now. There were three of them, and that spear had a far greater reach than Leonato's sword. It would pierce his breast and throw him down from Snowdrop in an instant.

I seized the closest thing at hand, a fallen branch no longer than my arm, and heaved it at the spearman. He hadn't been paying me heed, and the blow took him off guard. He staggered back. The stab of the spear went wild. Unfortunately, the axman had also charged Leonato. The prince blocked the blow, but the powerful recoil nearly unseated him.

I searched the mossy ground for another branch, a rock, a handful of acorns, but my fingers closed only on fistfuls of moldering leaves. I caught motion from the corner of my eye, and ducked, not quite in time. A dagger sliced past my cheek, sending a finger of fire along my shoulder. I cried out in pain and rage, kicking and flailing at my attacker. My foot struck something that crunched. Someone yowled in pain. Father's shoes remained sharp-heeled and sturdy as ever. I rolled back. Bits of dirt and leaf tangled in the loose hair that fell across my eyes. I brushed them aside and tensed for the next blow.

Snowdrop whinnied and filled the air with the stamp of his great hooves. Leonato sat atop the beast, battling furiously to keep back the two other brigands. Meanwhile, the man with the dagger crouched not six feet from me. Blood streamed from his nose, lending an even more fiendish look to his haggard features. "Ah, she's a little demon, she is," he said. "She shall need to be taught a lesson, then, shan't she? That pretty white skin will soon be tracked with red, red blood."

"Fortunata!" Leonato charged Snowdrop forward. The brigand staggered as the prince's blade caught him across the back. His gurgling scream prickled my skin, but I did not pause nor look. I scrambled up, keeping my back fast against the tree trunk.

Leonato wheeled Snowdrop around, reaching out. I caught his outstretched hand. He pulled me up behind him, even as the horse clattered along the trail. "Hold on!" he called. I needed no urging. I wrapped my arms tightly around Leonato as Snowdrop galloped on. The trees whipped past us, and the shouts of our attackers dwindled into weak, wordless roars.

The rush of trees was dizzying. I shut my eyes. I was

not aware of time passing, only the warmth of Leonato's strong back, the rise and fall of his chest under my embrace, the powerful surge of Snowdrop beneath us as he carried us away. Despite the peril behind us and the uncertainty ahead, I was at peace. Leonato and I were together, and that was all that mattered. "I think it's s-s-safe now," said Leonato.

I opened my eyes to find that we had stopped, though my heart continued to hammer. I realized I still had my arms wrapped tightly around the prince's torso. Quickly, I pulled free. "Your pardon, Highness."

"Be careful, you'll fall—"

I ignored his hand and slithered down from Snowdrop's high back. The ground was spongy with layers of mulching leaves, softening my fall. I looked around. The prince was correct that we were safe, from the brigands at least. But I could see no sign of anything familiar. Safe, but lost. Which was not exactly safe.

"Are we still on the trail?" I asked. My shoulder throbbed painfully.

"I don't know," he said, dismounting more gracefully than I had, to land lightly beside me. His eyes lighted on my shoulder in alarm. "Your sh-sh-shoulder. The monster cut you."

His look of concern melted away my pain for a moment. I craned my neck, trying to check the wound.

It felt like a brand across my shoulder, but I could at least still move my arm.

"Here, let me s-s-see." Leonato gently pushed aside my hands. His golden head bent near to mine as he examined the wound. He had the spicy scent of ferns and wet earth. "It's not a bad cut. I'll bind it up. I wish I had s-s-some woundwort."

"Perhaps we can borrow some from the witch," I said wryly, hoping to cheer both our spirits. I was rewarded with a quick grin from Leonato as he cut a strip from the hem of his wheat-colored shirt.

"Not many wounds get s-s-such a fine bandage, I'd bet," he said, looping the silk around my shoulder and tucking the loose ends. "It'll hurt, but I don't think it's deep enough to fester badly, if you keep it clean."

"Better than a slit throat. Thank you for saving me." I smiled. "I suppose it's good practice, for the princess. Saving other less worthy maidens from peril."

"You don't have to be a princess to be worthy." He took my hand, squeezing it tightly. "You s-s-saved me as well."

I knew in that moment why all the young lovers who listened to my lies believed me. I would have paid a gold coin for the certainty that Leonato would always gaze at me as he did then. I wanted someone to paint a bright future where we walked hand in hand. A future I could embrace, rather than fear. But all I had was that brilliant moment, so I clung to it, and to him. I likely could have stood there for quite some time, if I hadn't noticed a large white shape starting to edge off into the woods. "The horse!" I shouted, pulling my hand free from his.

Leonato sprang after Snowdrop, catching hold of the trailing reins just as the beast broke into a trot. The prince yanked the horse to a halt. Snowdrop turned his great head around to regard us with plain annoyance. He gave a snort and started forward again. "S-s-stop, you brute," Leonato said, barely holding the gelding back. "Where are you trying to go?"

"He knows the way," I said suddenly. "Back out of the forest. He can find our way out of here."

Leonato heaved on the reins, dragging Snowdrop back around to stand beside me. "All right, then. Up you go." He held out an arm as if to help me up, but I held back.

"The witch, my fortune—"

"Can wait. You're injured; that cut needs better tending. And S-saints know what's become of Captain Ribisi. We'll have to find the witch later."

"But . . ."

His jaw was set. I let my protest die away. At least I hadn't specified *when* the witch was to be defeated. Leonato was right. We had time.

Leonato insisted that I ride Snowdrop while he walked alongside. The prince remained tense, casting about for any sign of danger. He had Saint Federica's sword tight in one hand, the other wrapped around Snowdrop's reins. Once unhindered, the horse made his way peaceably.

What signs or instinct directed Snowdrop, I did not know. But clearly he knew exactly where he was going. His white ears remained pricked forward. He walked along unerringly, turning left or right on occasion, at no landmark I could see. I sighed, beginning to relax. My shoulder still ached. I decided that a hot meal and a cup of good wine would be most welcome before venturing back into these cursed woods.

"It's getting lighter," Leonato said. "I think we're nearing the edge of the forest." Snowdrop was nearly trotting now, so Leonato had to jog alongside. We broke through the last of the trees and out into the open. But it wasn't the edge of the forest. Tall oaks bounded the glade on every side. And in the center of the clearing stood a small cottage.

"The witch's house," Leonato said. "We've found it!"

I had to think quickly. Some innocent woodchopper might live here. And even if it was the old herb-woman I'd heard about, I still didn't want Leonato striking her down. "We must approach carefully," I said. "There may be magical spells protecting this place."

I scanned the grove. Besides the cottage itself, there was a small stable and a garden surrounded by a low stone wall. A few plump chickens scratched in the dirt near the stable, but that was the only sign of life. The cottage itself was a quaint old place, whitewashed pristinely under its peaked thatch roof. Two large diamond-paned windows flanked the front door, which was painted a bright blue, like cornflowers. Red and yellow roses climbed riotously over an archway that led into the garden. They cast a strong sweetness into the air. The place as a whole looked far too cheerful to be the home of a warty, evil old witch. But I would take what fortune the Saints had granted me.

I slipped down from Snowdrop's back. The horse set off instantly toward the stable. "It's as if he knows this place," Leonato said.

"Why should an old horse from Doma know of a cottage in the middle of the Black Wood?" I wondered aloud.

"But he's not just an old horse from Doma. He's the white s-s-steed from your prophecy."

"Oh, yes. That's right," I said, feeling my skin flush. If my prophecy had been true, I might have taken comfort in that.

We crept toward the side of the cottage, over a low hedge of lavender, and up to a small window. "I'll look," Leonato said. He held the sword of Saint Federica unsheathed and ready. His lips were set in a stern line as he edged up to the glass panes and peered within. "No s-s-sign of the witch, though it's crammed full with her magical potions and the tools of her dark— Wait! I s-s-see it!" He turned shining eyes back to me. "It's there, as you foretold."

He took my hand in his own, still holding the sword ready in the other, and led me around the corner to the blue door. As we entered, a riot of twittering and chirping filled the air. Leonato's grip tightened. We froze at the threshold. "Is it a s-s-spell?" Leonato asked.

"No, look." I pointed to the right wall of the cottage, where stood an array of what looked like small palaces built of twigs, filled with fluttering, winged forms. "Birds."

"Do you think they're poor s-s-souls, enchanted by the witch? I've heard tales of that." Leonato studied the cage, frowning.

"No," I assured him, for of course there was no such thing. "She probably just likes to hear them sing." They did make a sweet noise, as fair as any minstrel. "But we'd best get the slipper and be gone, before she returns." I looked about the rest of the large room.

It was crammed full of every leaf, root, flower, and tuber one could imagine. The rafters were thick with bunches of drying herbs, some fresh and green, others faded and dull. They stirred with the slight breeze that now whisked in through the open door, releasing a cascade of pungent scent. Across from us, a huge fireplace occupied almost the entire back wall. An iron cauldron nearly large enough to bathe in was set on the cold embers. Fresh kindling stood close by, stacked at the ready. Leonato pulled me around the huge table that occupied the center of the room. As I brushed against it, I saw a scattered pile of familiar silvery leaves beside a mortar and pestle.

"There, look," Leonato said, pointing up at a slightly crooked shelf.

He had said it was here, but I hadn't believed him. I had thought the prince had been seeing what he wished to see, like so many others. A copper bowl from a distance might look like a glittering gold slipper. But there it was. The twin of the shoe I had first seen in Doma, ornate with gems and glimmering even through a layer of dust. Leonato reached up to take it.

My thoughts whirled. My fortune was a lie. I had made it up. How, then, was this shoe here? I backed away, trembling, searching behind me for a stool or chair. I bumped up against something soft, and gave a yelp. I spun around.

"Thieves, is it?" the old woman cackled. She held up one crooked finger and shook it. "Tsk, tsk, you should know better than to try such things with old Grimelda, my dears."

"The witch!" Leonato cried, dropping the golden slipper as he sprang forward. "Get back, Fortunata." He grasped my shoulder, pulling me away from that wag-gling finger. He raised his sword, drawing himself up, shoulders back. "Her foul powers will not avail against the holy blade of Federica."

"Witch, am I?" said Grimelda, with a snort. "I prom-ise you this, boy, you steal from me and you'll find your-self under a spell quick enough. And you won't like it." She showed a mouthful of ragged teeth that looked frightfully like fangs. Leonato swallowed, but his sword did not falter. "Fortunata, get the s-s-slipper. We'll take pity on this creature and leave her with her life. It's not theft to take back what sh-she s-s-stole from my grand-mother."

Grimelda's brows rose up to the tangled thatch of gray curls that peeked out from under her brown cap. "Stole?" She gave her crow's caw of a laugh again. "Stole? You've got the story wrong, lad. So you're her grandson, are you? I suppose she was too ashamed to tell the true tale. But you'll not be taking that slipper."

I scooped up the golden shoe. Was the woman crazy, to stand so brazenly under the blade of Leonato's sword?

"My grandmother was no liar!" Leonato cried, his cheeks flushed. "S-s-stand aside!"

"That toy won't help you here, boy," she said, sniff-ing. Leonato gritted his teeth and swept the sword around in a warning cut between them. Grimelda moved more quickly than I could see.

The terrible clash made my bones rattle. I closed my eyes instinctively. When I opened them, I saw Leonato standing stricken, staring at the hilt of the sword in his hand. Only a hand span of the blade remained. It had shattered.

The old woman held up a large black frying pan and grinned. "You see, my loves, there's no blade can harm old Grimelda."

"But this was the holy blade," Leonato said. He looked at me. I felt as if my heart had stopped beating, or else that it hammered so fast I could not sense it. I had failed him.

I turned on Grimelda, full of fierce rage. She was not a witch; she couldn't be. My fortune was a lie. How dare she try to frighten us with threats of spells and magic? "You can't stop us!" I cried, brandishing the golden slipper.

"Foolish children," said Grimelda, shaking her head. She swept something up off the table beside her, and cast it at us. I coughed as a cloud of bitter dust filled the air. I batted at it, but the stuff clung to my nose, my lashes, my lips. My lungs burned. Tears sprang to my eyes. I was dimly aware of Leonato coughing, calling my name. Then the darkness swept over me and I knew no more.

CHAPTER

9

S OMEONE WAS SAYING my name. I blinked, blearily, but everything was gray and hazy. A pair of green eyes pierced that mist, bending close to my own. "Fortunata?"

I groaned. My head was cloudy and my shoulder ached terribly. I closed my eyes, but a pair of strong hands pulled me upright.

"Fortunata? Please, s-s-say s-s-something. Are you well?"

I opened my eyes, dragged out of my stupor by the fear in his voice. "Yes. Well enough. If the world would stop spinning." I concentrated on his face, and slowly the whirling ceased.

"Thank the S-s-saints. I thought the witch's s-s-spell had killed you." He squeezed my hand.

Witch's spell. I struggled to calm my racing heart. Had I been mistaken? I reviewed what had happened, searching for some explanation that did not involve a real witch springing to life out of my fabricated fortune. Grimelda had cast some sort of powder at me, at both of us. I'd fallen asleep, like Ubaldo after some of Allessandra's special nut cakes. I recalled the silvery leaves on the table. Dreamwell. That was it! The witch had simply poisoned us with a ground-up powder of the leaf. Put us asleep so that she might . . . what?

I looked past Leonato, trying to discover where we were. I could see the rafters and the bunches of herbs. It was darker than before. A lattice of woven branches crisscrossed my view in every direction. We were in a cage.

"Grimelda?" I asked.

"Not here. Not for s-s-some time."

"We've got to get out!" I said. I should have been overjoyed to have found the slipper and Grimelda, just as I had prophesied. But the truth was, it terrified me. I wanted to get as far from her as possible, before I started to believe anything more than herbcraft was at work here. I had to concentrate on Father, on getting the slipper and saving his life. This was no time to indulge in baseless fears about being turned into a toad or stewed up for dinner.

"I've tried to get out," said Leonato. "It's just

branches and vines, but I can't break them. The witch must have put a s-s-spell on them."

The cage was wide enough that we could both stretch out upon the floor, but not high enough for us to stand. It was a ramshackle, flimsy-looking thing, but when I tried the walls myself, I could not even twist loose the smallest twig. The gaps were only large enough to admit my hand, and a quick survey showed there were no useful implements within reach. The single square door was secured by two bright padlocks: one silver, one gold. Our cage was set up against one corner of the cottage, so that whitewashed walls stood behind and to our left. The hearth and table stood before us. A pair of blue jays, a crow, and several sparrows watched us with bright black eyes from the smaller cages to the right.

I rocked back onto my heels, telling myself it was simply a well-woven cage. Leonato had propped himself against the wall, knees drawn up. He drummed his fingers on the floor, which was cursed uncomfortable as it too was a lattice of branches and vines, atop the hard wooden floorboards. "Is it me?" he asked at last. "Is that why the s-s-sword didn't work? I'm not worthy to wield it, and now I've gotten you into this mess."

"Don't worry, Your Highness, we will escape," I said, trying to sound confident. After all, I knew Grimelda was no true witch. She had caught me off guard with the dreamwell, but there were two of us and one of her. We had only to break free. She wouldn't be able to stop us.

The door creaked open, and Grimelda trotted in with a sprightly bounce to her step. "Ah, awake are we? And all refreshed from the nice nap, my chicks?"

"What are you going to do with us, witch?" demanded Leonato, crawling forward to seize the branches of the door.

"Hmm . . ." Grimelda tilted her head consideringly. "What are witches supposed to do with little boys and girls they catch in the dark wood? Cook them up in a stew and eat them—that's the way of things."

A great lump formed in my throat as I saw that a bright fire had been lit in the hearth. Steam swirled up lazily from within the huge black cauldron. Leonato tugged at the branches, rattling the door and stirring up a cacophony of twitters and trills from the nearby cages.

"Now, now, young prince, you should know better than to try to tear that cage open with your bare hands. You're a strong lad, I see that, but my cage is stronger. There's but one way that door will open, and it's far beyond your grasp."

She gave a weird, ululating whistle. It was answered by twin fluting calls, as two small winged shapes fluttered down from the rafters. One perched on the peaked top of her cap, the other on her outstretched palm.

"Sweetbeak and Bitterwings will keep you safe and sound until I'm ready to deal with you naughty chicks, won't you, my dearies?" Grimelda smiled at the bluebird in her hand, and the expression lent an unexpected softness to her craggy face. The bird preened. I caught a golden glimmer of something hung around its neck, against the russet of its feathered breast. I squinted at the other bluebird, and saw it too bore a glittering pendant, but silver rather than gold. The keys.

Grimelda stalked to the hearth and took up a long wooden spoon to stir the contents of the cauldron. Sweetbeak and Bitterwings flew over to perch atop the shelf where the golden slipper had lain. "Perhaps I might take pity on you," Grimelda said, quirking one gray brow at us. "For I see you've returned something I lost long ago. And brought me the second slipper. That might set things to rights between us." She extracted something from a large pouch at her waist, and held it up. It was the pair of slippers, gems glinting in the firelight. She set them down on the table.

"What do you mean?" Leonato demanded. "Those s-slippers were my grandmother's. It's you who s-s-stole the one. And we brought you nothing."

"Snowdrop," I said suddenly. It all made sense now. I remembered the villagers talking about Queen Rosetta riding off into the forest on a black mare. But in the painting at the palace, she was riding a white horse during her escape. It was no wonder that Snowdrop had led us here. He was coming home.

Grimelda grinned. "Ah, sharp little chick. Yes, lovely Snowdrop. That wretched queen stole him away from me as well."

I frowned. "But that must have been forty years ago. He can't be that old, it's not possible."

"You'd be surprised how many things are possible, my dear." She reached up to tweak a few leaves from one of the bunches. She crushed them between her fingers, dusting the bits into the cauldron. The rich tang of sage filled the air, making my stomach grumble. "Now, then," she said, giving the contents another stir. "Let me tell you a story."

She pulled a chair out from the table and settled herself down. Sweetbeak and Bitterwings had fallen to squabbling over a spider or somesuch. After a spate of angry chirping, one of the two soared over to perch on her shoulder, twittering plaintively.

"It will be a true story, not the lies you've been told," Grimelda said. She produced a heel of dark bread from her tangle of robes and skirts and shawls. Breaking off a handful of crumbs, she scattered these upon the floor at her feet. Both birds swooped down at once to peck at the bits of bread.

"My grandmother told no lies!" Leonato insisted.

"Are you so certain? You never know what lies one

might tell, to protect oneself, or what one loves." She cocked her eye at me, and I shivered despite myself. No, that was ridiculous. This old woman could not possibly know anything about me.

"Your grandmother came to me seeking my help," Grimelda said, jabbing a bony finger at Leonato. "She wanted a child. The harvest had been meager, and the queen had been married five years and had borne no child. The people had begun to whisper that the kingdom was cursed. So she came to old Grimelda for a charm, on a horse as black as night, wearing slippers of gold."

Leonato was watching the woman intently, lips compressed, a challenging glint in his eyes. I was also listening, of course, but I was more concerned with the movements of the two birds. They were only just beyond reach. I could see the two small keys winking in the firelight as they bobbed their heads to peck up the crumbs.

"I told the queen I would give her my charm, and that she would bear not one child, but two. In exchange, she must give me her golden slippers. Well, she agreed. Swore by the Saints she would honor my price. I brewed the draught for her to drink, to settle the charm that would fill her womb. Down it went.

"Alas, she was a greedy woman. She threw down the glass and refused to yield the slippers. They were so lovely and fair she could not bear to part with them. Any other price, she offered. But we had made the deal, and I would not brook any change to it. She cried out then that she would not give me the shoes, and ran.

"She soon discovered that I had been tricksy, I had hidden her horse away. Without a mount, she could not escape. Yet she was a brave one, your grandmother. Greedy, but brave. She took my own horse, my Snow-drop, and made for the forest. As she rode away, one of the golden slippers fell from her foot. So it was I had half of my promised payment. Tell me, princeling, how many children did your grandmother bear?"

"Two," Leonato stated coolly. "But that doesn't mean I believe your s-s-story."

"Your father and another?" Grimelda prompted.

"His twin s-s-sister. My aunt."

"Your father, he would have been firstborn, then, of the pair. A good man, a good king."

Leonato's jaw unclenched and he nodded. "Yes, the best of men."

"You see, as your grandmother galloped away, I called out to her. I cursed her, in fact. I had granted her wish, and she would bear two children. I could not undo my charm, but I could twist it. The firstborn would be pure of heart and mind, noble and just. But the other would be cursed, wicked and cruel as a demon."

I gave a huff of surprise and glanced at Leonato. The

prince was pale, but the firm line of his lips admitted nothing.

Grimelda rocked back in her chair, chuckling. "Such a face, dear boy! You should be happy to hear you're of the good stock. It was all quite fair, I assure you. I even gave her the chance to give up the other shoe, and all would be forgiven. But she was a proud one too, and rode off thinking she could escape my curse as easy as she did my woods. Now, then, in all the gardens of your great palace, does there grow the yarrow plant?" She jabbed one finger up at the bundle of dried blossoms and leaves above her, the white flower heads browned, the long notched leaves curling. "Hmm?"

Leonato flicked a glance at me, and I knew he must be thinking of our conversation in the garden at the inn of Saint Federica's Rest. "No," he said. "Why?"

"Oh, just that yarrow has a baleful effect on demons. Your aunt wouldn't want to have it around, I'd imagine."

"My aunt can't be a demon," Leonato said. But there was a catch in his voice.

"Oh? Just because she's a lovely face and a sweet voice? Tell me, boy, what do you think of your aunt? Not her outsides. Think on her actions, her true nature." Grimelda's eyes were clever and dark as those of her bluebirds.

He did not speak for a long while, and the only sound was the flutter of wings and the tap of small beaks on the wooden floor. "Your curse worked," Leonato said at last. He pushed himself back from the gate abruptly and tucked himself against the wall again.

"Now, I've mushrooms to gather before night sets in. You chicks stay safe in your cage while I'm gone." Grimelda rose and hooked a large basket over one arm. She gave us a last snaggle-toothed grin and quit the room.

I WAS OF TWO minds to see her go. I could more easily effect our escape if she were gone. But it also meant I would be alone with Leonato, to explain how my prophecy had gone so horribly awry. When the door closed, I watched it for a long moment, loath to face the prince.

"Fortunata, how can we escape?" he said at last. "Do your visions tell you anything?"

I could only shake my head. Visions, hah. I rubbed my brow. My head still felt stuffed full of thistledown.

"Fortunata?" he asked, voice gentle as one might use to soothe a wild beast or a child. "Don't trouble yourself over the s-s-sword. It must be me."

"No," I said miserably, "it's not you. You've done everything right. It's my fault. I just can't see—" I stopped, aware that I teetered on the edge of a very deep chasm. But there was no way across.

"Maybe we didn't understand the vision," Leonato

suggested. "There must have been another weapon in Saint Federica's Rest, s-s-something we didn't even recognize. It isn't your fault."

Oh, but it is, I thought. Nevertheless, his words snapped me from the worst of my depression and gave me an idea. Some other weapon. I felt for the small pouch I carried at my waist. Saints be praised, it was still there. I had tucked the nut cake there yesterday. If we could nip some of the dreamwell from the table, perhaps I could trick Grimelda into a nice long nap.

But what I pulled from the pouch was a handful of crumbs. With all my tumbling and rolling and being attacked by the brigand, the cake had been crushed to bits. My heart fell.

"Fortunata, that's it!" Leonato said, staring at the bits of cake. "The weapon!"

"The weapon?" I looked at him blankly, wondering if the dreamwell had somehow driven the sense from his head.

"To defeat the witch. To get the keys," he explained. He cupped my hand with his own, turning it so that he caught the crumbs. Kneeling by the front of the cage, he reached out through the bars and scattered them close by.

I understood. Quickly I dumped the rest of the cake bits from my pouch into a pile just inside the cage. I looked around the cottage for the birds. They had demolished the bread crumbs Grimelda had left them earlier, then flitted up into the rafters. I had not seen them fly after her. I gave an experimental whistle.

This set the birds in the cages into a cacophony, but I thought I heard the delicate chirp of one of the bluebirds from above. "There," Leonato said, pointing to a bundle of love-in-a-mist that was swaying slightly. Two swift blue shapes dove down, landing with a series of excited twitters.

They were pretty little fellows, with their brilliant blue backs and russet breasts. I held myself still as stone, fearful of startling them. After cocking their heads left, then right, then left, the two bluebirds hopped forward and set to work on the crumbs.

"I'll take the gold," Leonato said. "Can you handle the s-s-silver?"

I nodded, afraid even to speak. My hands were hot and slick. I hoped I could hold the tiny creature. The bluebirds gobbled up the crumbs, occasionally pausing for a squabble over the choicest bits of sugared nut. At last they had passed between the bars. They were only a foot from the edge of my skirts when Leonato hissed, "Now!"

I grabbed for the bird nearest me, the one with the tiny silver key trembling against his russet breast. I felt as if I had grabbed a handful of falling petals, the creature was so fragile beneath my fingers. I tried to handle it gently, but I could not risk losing the key. The bird chirped with agitation, rousing the others in the cottage to even more riotous commotion.

Leonato grunted, but he held his hands cupped gingerly before him, and wore a triumphant grin. "Got it!" he said. Carefully he tightened one hand and released the other, so that he held the bird neatly in one hand. He tweaked the tiny gold chain from around the bird's head and released it.

I followed his example, and we soon had two keys in hand, and two angry bluebirds fluttering about the rafters and sending down showers of dried leaves. "Quickly!" I said. "She could return at any time!" I had given up trying to convince myself Grimelda wasn't a witch. I knew she had no magic, just herbcraft. But she made shivers creep along my spine, and I wanted to be as far away from her as I could be.

Leonato reached between the branches, bending his wrist to fiddle with the padlocks. A moment longer, and we were free. Leonato started for the door. "The slippers," I cried, darting back to the table. I snatched them up, and we flew out the door.

WE FLED ON FOOT, not daring to seek out Snowdrop. Besides, I was not sure we would be able to convince the horse to leave, if this was truly his home. The sky above the glade was silver-gray, with a hint of pink in the west. Night came fast. We ran past the thick pillars of the trees, our feet making no sound upon the carpet of leaves. Darkness pressed in closely, slowing our progress. Though there was little undergrowth, the twisting roots of the great oaks covered the ground, ready to catch our unwary steps. Every weird hooting, every rustle of branches sent prickles marching along my back.

I lost track of time, knowing only the endless stumbling, the warm clasp of Leonato's hand, and the loud rush of my own gasping breaths. Then a prick of light sparkled suddenly, off in the blackness ahead. It was gone in a blink, behind a distant tree perhaps, but I had fixed the direction. I pulled Leonato toward it. "A light!"

"A lamp?"

"By the Saints, I hope so," I said fervently. My whole body ached; each step jarred my cut shoulder, wrapping a band of fire around it.

"I s-s-see it," he said. I could not see his face any longer, but his voice was hopeful.

We oriented on the wink of yellow and quickened our pace. The trees grew sparser and smaller, and the darkness gradually lessened. We were closing in on the light, and now I could see that it was moving. It had a trembling reddish gold cast to it. A torch.

"Leonato!" a deep voice bellowed.

I felt Leonato start beside me, then quicken his pace still further. "Captain Ribisi!" We burst from the edge of the wood, out into the starlit fields. Captain Ribisi's face was lit by the torch he carried, cast into fiendish shadows and angles.

My heart grew chill as I remembered when we had last left him. He had led us into the woods, right into the heart of an ambush, and abandoned us. What was to stop him from finishing the job now? I started to stammer something, to pull Leonato back, but he let go of my hand and ran to the captain.

Captain Ribisi wrapped one arm around the boy and hugged him close. "My prince, thank the Saints you're safe." For a moment, in the torchlight, I could see his eyes. They were squeezed tightly shut, his mouth puckered into a trembling line. Then he pushed Leonato back away from him. Captain Ribisi passed one hand across his face, but when he looked up the grim, stoic mask was back as ever before.

I blinked, not certain I had truly seen the relief and emotion that had been there. And even if I had, I told myself, I knew that such things could be manufactured. I had wept and wailed often enough as a spirit for Allessandra. But my hammering heart slowed a bit. Whatever secret he had, the captain did not appear intent on harming the prince at the moment.

"And you, Captain, did those monsters in the wood harm you?"

"The brigands? No. But when I chased off the archers and returned to the trail to find you gone, and no track to follow, I cursed myself to the seven Hells. And when the girl's donkey returned riderless, I feared the worst."

"There were three more. They attacked us. I would have died on the s-s-spear of one, but Fortunata s-s-saved me. We ran, only trying to escape—but Captain, we found the witch, and the s-s-slipper!"

Captain Ribisi's brows rose. "Is that so? Well, you can tell me the whole tale when you're fed and tended."

We passed the remainder of the night in a tiny hamlet south of the wood, crammed into the small house of the wealthiest farmer. As I lay on my pallet, hearing the captain's snores and Leonato's slow breaths from the other room, I considered the events of the last few days. I could not quite wrap my thoughts around them. I turned on my side, then my back, trying to ease the ache of my sore shoulder, now covered in a sticky green paste from the apothecary and wrapped in fresh bandages. Somehow, with luck and by the whims of the Saints, I had managed to get through most of my fortune. But the hardest part still lay ahead. Oh, finding a girl to fit the slippers did not trouble me. But we must go to Sirenza, into the domain of Captain Niccolo. My heart shrank at the thought of meeting him again. I comforted myself that if all went well, I would not have to. We could slip in, find the first girl to fit the shoes, and whisk her away back to Doma, where she could marry Leonato and live happily ever after.

A wave of hot jealousy flashed through me. I flopped onto my stomach, then my side again, but I couldn't stop the painful images that flooded my mind. Visions of Leonato and a girl in golden slippers, passing under the crossed boughs in a grand cathedral. The pair of them riding through sun-dappled fields, the prince handing his beloved a posy of wildflowers. Leonato embracing this faceless false princess, smiling at her the way he had—

I closed my eyes, drawing up the memory of Leonato telling me I didn't have to be a princess to be worthy. I could almost smell the spicy fern scent of him, feel the warmth of his hand holding mine. In that moment, I had been sure he did not want some unknown princess. In that moment, I had dared to believe in a bright and shining future of my own.

I heaved a shuddering breath, dragging myself back from that dangerous, heavenly thought. It didn't matter what I felt. My father needed me now, more than ever. My gentle father, with his shy smile and quick delight. How happy he'd been to see the paintings in the palace; he loved beauty so. And he would have beauty of his own again. I would do whatever it took. I would even clean his tools as Mother had. If he needed fairies, I would give him fairies. If only I could see this through, to make my fortune come true. Then we could leave Doma and Ubaldo and all of this behind. Even if it meant leaving Leonato too . . .

CHAPTER

10

OUR LONG, SLENDER BOAT slipped across the dark waters of the Balta toward the glittering cluster of lights that was Sirenza. I sat at the prow, my cloak pulled tight around my shoulders against the wind that scudded down the water from the north. It could not protect me from the chill that blew through my heart, now that we were so close to the end.

It had taken us two weeks to reach Sirenza. In my mind, those days were lit with an endless golden sunlight, filtering across the green fields we had ridden through, scattered with sunflowers and poppies. I had steadfastly avoided any thought of the future. Instead, I had stored up memories, like fat golden coins I would hoard for the rest of my life.

The memory of Leonato dancing me around a dusty village square when we happened upon a celebration of the feast of Saint Aleppo. I had been embarrassed, out of practice, but he had been too jubilant to care if I stumbled. Soon enough, I didn't care either.

The memory of huddling under the leaky overhang of some shepherd's barn, waiting out a sudden storm. I should have been wretched, soaked, and shivering. But Leonato found a kindle of kittens in the hay, and before I knew it, even dour Captain Ribisi was smothering a smile at their antics.

The prince had a boundless capacity for delight and shared it freely. When I was with him, I loved life with a joy I had not felt in many years. My past might hold sorrows, my future might be uncertain, but for those two weeks I had a glorious, sunlit present.

But I could ignore the future no longer. The paddles dipped softly into the rippling waters as Leonato and the captain rowed us smoothly toward Sirenza. She was there, somewhere. The girl that Leonato would marry. I felt ill. I peered at the prince, trying to discern what he might be feeling. Was he excited? Did his heart pound at the thought of his mystery bride? I knew we had no future together, but that did not stop me from wanting to know if Leonato regretted it as much as I.

I comforted myself that he looked troubled, before I

remembered the first rule of fortune-telling: People believe what they want to believe. Even me. Bitterly, I tore my gaze from the prince and concentrated on the city ahead.

We drifted in with a line of other vessels passing into the main canal. Two great braziers burned on stone pilings at either side of the canal entrance. A barge held fast in the center, and on it stood a cluster of guards. As each boat passed into the city, it drew up alongside the barge. I peered through the night, trying to make out the faces of the guards, but the leaping flames of the brazier made it hard to see their features.

We were nearly upon it, with only a large skiff ahead of us, when I got a good look at the men on the barge. I shrank down instantly, with a muffled yelp.

"What's wrong?" Leonato called in a low voice.

"It's the Bloody Captain himself," I hissed. "There on the barge."

"Don't worry. He has no reason to trouble with us."

We had agreed to travel in the guise of a minor landowner and his two children, on pilgrimage to the statue of Saint Marco in the grand plaza of Sirenza. But Captain Niccolo would see through this ruse the moment he set eyes on me. "He knows me," I admitted. "He'll know I'm not a pilgrim."

Captain Ribisi moved so nimbly he barely rocked the

boat, passing Leonato his own oar, and hastening forward to the prow. "Keep your hood up," he ordered, and shoved me none too gently toward the side of the boat that faced away from the barge. "And keep quiet."

The guards were calling us to draw up. Leonato dipped both oars into the water. He frowned, whether in concentration or concern I didn't know. But he gave me a reassuring grin when he caught me looking at him.

"Keep your face down," ordered Captain Ribisi. His iron grip held me fast against the far side of the boat, so I couldn't see what was happening. I heard the creak of the barge under booted feet, heard the rote questions. Captain Ribisi gave his false name and supposed business and place of origin. When he announced that we were from Saint Federica's Rest, the guard said, "Lord Niccolo, these ones are northerners. Would you like to question them yourself, sir?"

I nearly lost my dinner over the side of the boat. The stamp of well-heeled boots approached.

"Northerners, are they?" Niccolo's voice slid cold fingers along my spine. Part of me wanted to turn around, to see if he was looking at me, if he had somehow recognized me. Another part wanted to leap then and there into the canal, though I could not swim. Anything to get away from him. "Your names?"

"Giorgio, my lord, and my children, Federico and Maria."

"Bring that lantern," said Niccolo, and from the corner of my eye I saw a beam of golden light sweep over our boat. "Fine-looking lad, though nothing of your coloring in that hair."

"He takes after his mother, my lord."

"And your daughter?"

Captain Ribisi's hand tightened on my shoulder. "I'm afraid she's not taken well to travel by boat, my lord."

I followed his hint and dutifully began producing wretched sounds as I leaned out farther over the side. It was not far from the truth.

"Tell me, Master Giorgio, in your travels south have you come across a northern prince and his entourage? They would be traveling south as well."

"No, my lord."

There was a long pause. I feared we had somehow been discovered. Had Coso come south from Doma to warn the captain? I held my breath. "Very well. You may go about your business. My man will take the entrance tax." Then the boots clicked against the barge, retreating. Captain Ribisi removed his hand from my shoulder, though I remained clinging to the side of the boat.

"That's five guilders," said one of the guards.

As Captain Ribisi rummaged in our bags to find the payment, I could hear Niccolo muttering to his other men. "Come to find the princess, curse it. How they discovered she was here I do not know. If there have been loose lips, they will soon be cut. . . ."

"There's no way anyone could free her, my lord, not from the tower."

"There should have been no way for anyone to know she yet lived," said Niccolo, his voice rising. "You lot stay alert. You're to let me know if any other travelers from the north pass through. And double the watch boats. I want no one entering or leaving the city without my knowledge. Is that clear?"

The hearty affirmations rang across the canal as we rowed on under the bridge and into the Grand Canal of Sirenza. As the barge passed into darkness behind us, I turned from the side of the boat, not certain I could believe this stroke of good fortune.

"Did you hear?" Leonato asked. "What luck! The S-s-saints are truly s-s-smiling on us."

"That captain's an idiot," was all Captain Ribisi said.

"So we need to find this tower," said Leonato. He paused, frowning into the heart of the city. "And rescue the princess."

I wondered if it was the challenge of extracting a prisoner from the Bloody Captain's grasp that made the prince look so bleak. Or was it something more? Oh, how I dreaded and yearned for the faceless princess. She was the key to my greatest happiness and my deepest sorrow. Find her, and I would save my father's life. Find her, and I would lose Leonato to her forever.

I jerked myself out of these dark thoughts. I was being an idiot. I didn't have Leonato, so how could I lose him? I shouldn't question this good luck. But still my brain whirled, like a restless, feverish child. There were things going on I did not understand. Yet, whatever else, I had the means to make my fortune come true. That was all that really mattered. Father's life depended on it.

WE TOOK ROOMS at a small inn near the great cathedral, middling accommodations suited to our supposed station. Leonato was all afire to start investigating possible locations of "the tower," but Captain Ribisi had other ideas. We were playing the parts of pilgrims, and so we must do what pilgrims would do: Visit the statue of Saint Marco in the grand plaza and attend the Mass of Saints at the cathedral.

"We risk drawing unwelcome attention otherwise," he cautioned as we took our breakfast the morning after our arrival, on a balcony that jutted out over the Grand Canal. He set a slim book in a tattered leather cover down on the table, between the basket of bread and the bowl of oranges.

"The verses of Saint Marco?" I guessed. A pilgrim would almost certainly be carrying such a thing.

He nodded, and passed us each a string of glass beads. "And prayer beads as well," I said. I had to respect the captain, though I was still suspicious of him. He was as clever as I in deception. I held up the necklace, admiring the flashes of amber and green in the sunlight.

"All these lies," Leonato said, setting the handful of beads down so roughly I feared he might break them. "I don't like it."

I felt as small and tattered as the prayer book. I had been deceiving the prince for weeks, and my lies were far worse than a false name and a string of beads. Sudden dread filled me like a brimming cup of poison. Leonato must never know. I could lose him to a beautiful princess, but I could never bear to have him look on me with disdain and disgust. "The most important thing is to rescue the princess," I said, forcing myself back to the matter at hand. "That is your task. Even with an army you couldn't take this city without great bloodshed, and the captain might well murder the girl."

"Is that what you s-see?" Leonato asked, twisting a rind of orange in his fingers, filling the air with the sharp citrus scent.

"It's what the captain would do," I said. Even without magical foresight, I knew Captain Niccolo was that sort of man.

Leonato cast aside the scrap of peel and took up the

prayer beads moodily. He slipped the string around his neck. "Then pilgrims it is."

I WAITED WITH Captain Ribisi in the shadow of Saint Marco, who stood tall and bronze as if ready to spring up into the heavens. The prince was mingling with the crowds leaving the cathedral, hoping to hear something useful about the princess amid the chatter and gossip. I was keeping my eye on Captain Ribisi. I still had my doubts about his loyalties and couldn't afford to give him the chance to contact our enemies.

Clouds of pigeons swirled over our heads, flocking to an old man and his grandson, who were feeding them stale bread near the fountain. Captain Ribisi watched them inscrutably for a long moment, then deposited a garland of roses at the sandaled feet of the statue, his gray head bent low. I wondered what prayers he muttered to the Saints, over his posy of remembrance.

When I saw Leonato approaching, I assumed from his troubled expression that he had learned nothing. He thumped himself down beside the statue, gripping the bench on either side, as if bracing himself. "I've found out where she is." He stared toward the Royal Canal that ran along the far side of the plaza. "There's a tower in the north quarter, near the palace. They call it the Perdutto, the tower of the lost."

"Not a promising name," I said.

"But you've s-s-seen that I would rescue the princess in your visions. I'll find a way," Leonato said, intently. "I must."

And I must help him. I forced myself to think of my father, of how we would travel once he was free, singing the silly journey songs he loved, finding the best nut cakes in every town and village. We might even return to Valenzia. Perhaps I would buy him a Bragelli painting of his own. There should be enough from what I would earn deceiving Leonato. I knew I could never spend a penny of it on myself.

Captain Ribisi rose, flicking a stray petal from his sleeve. "Trust in your own strength, not visions, my prince. Now, let's go take a look at this tower."

We hired a gondola at the edge of the plaza, for travel to the north quarter was a circuitous and tangled route on foot, according to Captain Ribisi. The gracefully curved vessel slipped through the green waters of the Royal Canal, the gondolier chanting in time with his poling and calling out greetings to his brethren.

The captain had us disembark not far from the palace, past a narrow footbridge that spanned the canal. I could see men and women leaning out their windows, chatting amiably across the gap between them. Two boys were poling a small raft from door to door, delivering baskets of lemons. Captain Ribisi led us up a stone stair to a narrow walk that ran atop several buildings, green and fragrant with rooftop gardens.

"You know this city well," I remarked as the older man took us down another flight of steps I had nearly missed.

"It was once my home," he said.

I shared a look with Leonato, who appeared as surprised as I at this admission. "Why did you leave?" asked the prince.

But just then we emerged into a sort of cloister along the edge of a larger body of water. "There," said Captain Ribisi simply.

There was no question what he meant. A single finger of stone rose from the water, smooth and seamless, as if it were a great boulder carved by the hands of the Saints into this cylinder. It stood separate from any other structure, surrounded on all sides by the softly riffled waters. The canal widened out into nearly a small lake here. On the far edge, colorful banners flapped from the balconies of a row of white buildings.

"What's on the other side?" I asked.

"The Collegium," Captain Ribisi said. "Those are the colors of the student societies."

"And this side?" I peered up along the covered walk at the massive stone masonry rising beyond.

"It was once the Hall of Kings, but it's been turned

over to the Bloody Captain's soldiers, for use as barracks."

Leonato paid no heed to our exchange. He stood at the edge of the walk, where a low stone wall bounded us from the waters below. "Look. There's s-s-someone at that window. It must be her, the princess." He leaned out over the stone wall so far I feared he might tumble down into the canal.

I frowned, squinting at the window. A pale oval, blurred by the distance, but set in a sweep of gold that trailed down the gray stone casement. She was too far away for me to tell, but I had a strange foreboding that she was beautiful. Probably with ruby lips and eyes of cornflower blue, to go with that cornsilk hair. Impractically long, I thought derisively. Why, it must be down to her knees. My own brown braids fell only to the middle of my back, though normally I wore them coiled atop my head out of the way.

"Is sh-sh-she beautiful?" Leonato asked, still staring at the window.

I coughed. "What?"

"The princess, you must have s-s-seen her in your visions. I was, well, wondering if sh-she was beautiful. It's not required by the Edicts, of course. I was just . . . curious."

I struggled with my throat, which had gone suddenly tight and dry. Leonato deserved someone beautiful, and kind, and intelligent. And truthful. "I don't know," I said at last. I turned to study the Collegium banners as I spoke, unable to face him. "That is, I saw only her feet. In the vision. We'd better try to get around to see that tower on the other side."

IN THE END, our plan was a relatively simple one. The guards at the Perdutto were as regular in their rounds and watches as the moon circling the heavens. Captain Ribisi and Leonato spent a long night observing the pattern and found a flaw that we could turn to our advantage. Between the first dark watch and the midnight change, there was a short period when the lowest window, not two man-heights from the canal, was unobserved. If we were prepared to move quickly, we could get a small boat to the window and back in that time. There were so many variables I froze with fear if I began to consider them. What if the girl was too slow, what if someone else happened by, what if the guards altered their routine?

But it was our best option. I had given up worrying about whether the slippers would fit. We would get her out and then see. And if they didn't, Saints help me if I didn't chop the girl's toes off to make them fit.

We waited in the shadow of a balcony jutting out from the Collegium. I could just make out snippets of a debate within, over some obscure philosophical point in the writings of Saint Humberto. Captain Ribisi crouched like a gargoyle at the edge of our raft, motionless, the silvery glints in his hair pricked out by the starlight. Thankfully the crescent moon overhead was dim, but I still felt that we would be terribly exposed in this undertaking. What if Leonato was spotted by the guard and shot? What if he fell?

"Stop fidgeting, both of you," Captain Ribisi ordered. "It's nearly time."

Leonato slid the dagger he'd been fiddling with back into the scabbard at his belt. I stood up from the ledge that ran along the canal, realizing I had been drumming my fingers on the stone. The night darkened. A cloud had swarmed over the moon.

"Now!"

Leonato took up the pole and pushed us off into the lazy current. I held my breath as we drifted along in the darkness, praying the cloud would remain. I looked along the top of the barracks across from us, but saw no sign of the guard. We had until he completed his circuit of the walkway to finish our task. Captain Ribisi took hold of his own pole and worked with the prince to guide us toward the Perdutto.

We bumped up against the smooth stone with a thump that made my heart stutter. Even out here I could hear the laughter of the students floating over the dark water. The canal seemed to magnify all sounds. I kept my eyes fast on the edge of the barracks, expecting to see a guard at any moment.

Someone tapped my arm. I looked up to see Captain Ribisi holding out one of the poles. I took it, nodding. My part was to keep the raft from slipping free and continuing on along the canal. The current held us pushed up against the tower for now, but shortly Leonato and the captain would be too occupied with other things to tend to the raft.

I thrust the end of the long length of wood down into the water, into the squelching silt below. Captain Ribisi hastened to position himself against the side of the tower, hands interlaced, ready to give Leonato a leg up to the window above. The prince scrambled up gracefully, caught hold of the window ledge, then pulled himself up to balance lightly for a moment before jumping down inside. His blond head reappeared briefly as he gave us a reassuring wave, then he was gone.

I felt as if a great weight sat squarely upon my chest, crushing the air from me. My hands gripping the pole were slick with sweat. I rubbed first one, then the other against my skirts as the moments crawled past. It was the guard's imminent arrival that made me fret—that's what I told myself. I had no reason to care what was going on in the tower. I had read enough fairy tales. It would be love at first sight probably. Or he would find her sleeping (in a bower of silk and flowers no doubt) and wake her with a kiss. Would he think of me at all? I wondered. Would he feel any regret? Or was it only I who felt this brutal rip tearing through my heart? Ruthlessly, I crammed the thoughts into the back of my mind. This was his destiny. I had made it so.

When it came, the rustle of movement above nearly sent me out of my skin. Captain Ribisi had remained stationed below the window. He reached up as a cloud of misty white silk and ribbons descended from the window. The girl gave a mewling scream. I ground my teeth, holding fast to the pole as Captain Ribisi caught the girl and helped her down. I could see Leonato's blond head. He lowered himself, then fell lightly to the raft.

Even braced against the tower, the raft rocked somewhat. I heard another scream, though this one was somewhat muffled. Wonderful. It couldn't have been a sensible princess who would understand that rescue from dire peril demanded silence. "Shh!" I hissed to the girl. "Do you want them to know you've escaped?"

She turned around, and I saw with a sinking heart that she was all I had feared. Beautiful as a flower, fragile as the dawn. Fit to inspire a hundred minstrels. Her eyes were large, and one small white hand pressed to her lips in a childish gesture of embarrassment. "Oh!" she said. "But my prince will save me from any danger." She turned adoring eyes upon Leonato, who even now had taken up his pole again and was helping Captain Ribisi direct the raft back to shore. The prince glanced up long enough to smile. He looked bewildered, but whether by love or confusion I could not tell.

I suppressed the desire to throttle the girl. My heart thrummed in my ears. Father's life depended on my fortune coming true, and for that I needed a princess. This one not only looked the part, clearly she had fallen for Prince Leonato already. But what did *he* think of *her*?

I tried to concentrate on watching the barracks roof, but I was acutely aware of how beautiful the girl looked in her white nightgown, those long tresses loose, draping her in a shimmering, cornsilk cloak. Misery stabbed through me. How had I ever dreamed Leonato might feel anything for me? This was the sort of ethereal, lovely creature he deserved. She might not be particularly useful in a dangerous situation, but she was real and true. I was just a liar trying to save my father's life.

I wrenched my eyes away from both Leonato and the girl, and turned to observe the approaching Collegium promontory. The scholars in the chamber above had fallen silent, or gone out, and the lamps had been darkened. But what was that? A dark shape on the balcony ahead, crouched beside the fluttering banner. I squinted, trying to make it out. Had it been there before? Was it a potted plant, or decorative statuary?

Then the darkness turned silvery. The moon emerged

from the veiling clouds. I saw the shape clearly; a shaft of moonlight lit a slender curve of wood. Just barely I heard the twang, but I was already moving.

"Down!" I hissed, throwing myself at the princess, pulling her down to the raft. "Archer!"

She gave another scream as she collapsed. The shaft went keening through the air, to embed itself in the wood of the raft just past where I lay in a tangle with the princess. The raft changed course, as Leonato and Captain Ribisi began poling us away from the assailant.

"Stop whimpering," I ordered the girl, tearing off my cloak and casting it over her. In that white gown she was as fair a target as the moon itself. She batted at my hands, and I received a sharp elbow in my ribs that seemed fairly deliberate. But I had more important concerns now.

A cry rose from the far side of the Perdutto, answered by another from atop the barracks. Another twang, but the second arrow splished harmlessly into the canal. Lights appeared along the barracks, bobbing in the hands of running guards.

"They've seen us," Captain Ribisi said. "We must reach that covered walk. The Collegium isn't safe with the archer there. Quickly, my prince."

We were not far from the other side of the canal now, but I could see the line of lanterns trailing down, moving that way. More lights bobbed out across the canal, as guards in boats of their own began rowing after us. Another arrow hissed past, and Leonato grunted. "I'm all right," he said, before I could even ask. "Just s-sliced my s-s-sleeve."

Muffled wails came from under my cloak as the princess tried to push the dark wool off herself. "No, Princess, stay there, you'll be seen," I said, trying to prevent her from casting the entire cloak into the canal. As I leaned close, another hard elbow jabbed at me, this time catching my chin. The blow sent me reeling back.

I had one glimpse of the jeweled stars above before I crashed down into frigid water. It closed in around me with a horrible heavy pressure, slowing my frenzied flailing, pulling down, down, down on my sodden gown. I struggled, trying to claw for the edge of the raft. But my fingers felt only the empty cold water. My chest burned, until I opened my mouth to scream. Then a great rushing cold filled me, pushing into my throat, my nostrils, my ears. I could see no light at all.

Had the Saints finally come to claim me for my deceptions? A fitting end, slain by the very princess I had made up. If only my last sight didn't have to be that beautiful, stupid, heedless princess.

The darkness became complete.

CHAPTER

11

I WOKE TO SOMEONE prodding my shoulder. The dagger wound from the Black Wood had mostly healed, but that spot was still somewhat sore, and I flinched. I blinked the crusty sleep from my eyes, grunting in surprise. The light in the room was dim, but still far too bright for night. And what was I doing in a room in any case? We had been on the canal, fleeing with the princess, when I had fallen into the water.

"Awake?" demanded someone near my head.

"Ouch!" I cried as my shoulder was poked again. I craned my neck to see the person seated beside my bed. By daylight, the princess was even more beautiful. She looked vaguely familiar, but perhaps that was because she resembled one of the carved Saints. Her skin was as translucent and fine as rose petals. Her eyes, to my surprise, were hazel, not blue. But in all other respects, she was exactly what I expected. Only the petulant pursing of her red lips and the crease between those delicately arched golden brows marred her full beauty.

"I'm awake," I said, flinching as she prepared to jab me again. "Where am I? What happened?" I pushed myself up. This did not look like my room in the inn. It was a rougher, simpler chamber. Then the door opened to admit Leonato.

"You're awake? Thank the S-s-saints," he said, hastening to the bedside. His smile warmed me as much as the princess's glower chilled.

"Oh, my prince, you should not be troubling yourself over the girl," cooed the princess, leaning forward to interpose herself between Leonato and the bed. "You've been through such an ordeal, you must rest and recover your own strength."

My initial irritation was lost in a stronger wave of fear. I looked him up and down for signs of illness or injury. "What ordeal? Are you hurt, Leonato?"

"Your Highness," corrected the princess, but I did not even spare her a scowl.

"Princess Maridonna is most generous in her concern, but I'm fine, Fortunata. It's you I was worried about, drinking down half the Royal Canal."

"Oh, the girl's well enough," Maridonna said. "She's

from hearty peasant stock. Look at those red cheeks. Such folk are used to hardships."

The redness in my cheeks had little to do with good health, but I bit down the furious words that threatened to burst out. After all, I needed the princess to make my fortune come true. I couldn't afford to insult her. Unfortunately, I seemed to offend her simply by existing.

The door opened again. I stared in amazement at the figure standing there. Had my dunking somehow fevered my brain?

"Allessandra! What are you doing here?"

She smiled, a more open and true smile than any I had seen on her face. It softened the sharpness of her features, as did the cheerful rose scarf and nut-brown gown, so different from the severe brilliance of her costumes. "I might ask you the same, child. This is my house."

I looked between Allessandra and Leonato. "How . . . ?"

"As I understand it, this lad fished you out of the canal half-drowned. I found him with my father and the lady here trying to revive you. So I took you all here, to my house. You've had a good dunking but no lasting harm."

"Your father?" I wondered if there was still canal water clogging my ears. I blinked as Captain Ribisi followed her into the room. His dour expression lightened as he looked at Allessandra. He hugged her gently to him, like a man cupping a flickering candle, fearful that he might extinguish it.

"Captain Ribisi is your father?" I turned my stunned eyes to Allessandra. "He's the father who sold you to Ubaldo?"

Captain Ribisi tightened his grip on Allessandra. She patted his hand and spoke quickly. "No, it was a lie. It was all lies. Ubaldo deceived me into thinking that, to keep me with him. Just as my father was deceived—"

"Curse that man to the seven Hells," Ribisi said, his face very red. "He stole her from me, and she was all that I had."

"Shush, Father. It's done and over." Allessandra leaned into his embrace, tears glinting at the corners of her eyes. She brushed them away. "Now I've found you again. And as the Saints will it, I have the means to be of assistance to you."

I sat back against the bolster, my thoughts whirling.

"The girl is tired, we should leave her in peace," Maridonna said sweetly. She rose from her chair, holding out one slender hand so that Leonato was obligated to assist her. Once she had his hand, she clung to it, pulling him toward the door. "Should we not be making plans to leave the city? You must be crowned, my prince. And we must be married."

That pulled my thoughts into sharp and painful clarity. "Married?"

"Yes, Leonato has told me all about the Edicts and your wonderful prophetic visions. They led him to me, to rescue me from this foul place." Maridonna gazed up through a veil of golden lashes at Leonato, who looked a trifle flushed.

"So, you've tried on the slippers? They fit?" I asked. My heart beat loudly in my ears. I didn't know what answer I hoped for.

"Yes, lovely things they are. I shall have a gown made to match, to wear for our wedding." Maridonna sidled closer to Leonato, still keeping a firm hold of his hand. The prince watched me with an odd look I could not interpret, for all my experience in reading faces.

"Oh. Well," I said, lamely. "Good. Then the fortune is fulfilled."

"Nearly," said Captain Ribisi. "But we're still in Sirenza, and there are at least two enemies arrayed against us. The Bloody Captain's guards, and that archer and whatever others he might be in league with."

"We have to leave at once, before they discover us here." I pushed down the blanket, then clutched it back up, realizing that I was garbed in nothing but a thin chemise.

"Here are your clothes," Allessandra said, gently pulling away from Captain Ribisi and picking up a blue bundle from the corner of the room. "Washed and dried. Tomas has a nice platter of sausage and cabbage for dinner. Why don't you all go and eat. Fortunata and I will join you shortly."

Maridonna wasted no time in pulling Leonato out into the hall. "I'm glad you're all right, Fortunata," he said, pausing at the door.

"Thank you," I said. "Thank you for rescuing me." But Leonato was already gone, and I was alone with Allessandra.

I felt as if I had fallen into a dark and lonely pit, and could not call for help. I tore my gaze from the closed door and turned to Allessandra. "Who's Tomas?" There were so many questions I wanted to ask, but I started with the most recent.

"My husband." She grinned at my surprise. "Yes, Allessandra the All-Knowing has become Allessandra Grappa, the candlemaker's wife. Though it was a long road back. . . ." She dropped her eyes to the blue dress she still held.

"I'm glad you left," I said. I remembered how furious I had been, but now that I saw her here, happy, peaceful, I could find no embers of that old anger.

She looked up, eyes wide and searching. "You forgive me for leaving you there, with him?"

"He had Papa's gold chain," I said. "I would have stayed anyway. You had to leave. I'm glad you did."

"Thank you," she said simply. "But I am going to do all that I can to aid you now. I've heard some of the story from my father and Prince Leonato. You have made a prophecy, I hear?"

"Yes, and if it doesn't come true, Papa will be executed. He swore I had the True Sight," I explained miserably. Then the words were tumbling out of me. It was a relief to share the tale with someone.

"Though I don't know how it came to be that Grimelda really was there with the shoe and all, and that there truly was a princess here in Sirenza. I suppose the Saints have taken pity on me and Papa," I finished.

"And the prince and my father suspect nothing?"

"Your father doesn't believe in magic," I said. "Not since you were taken from him." My fears about the captain hung at the tip of my tongue, but I could not speak them. Allessandra was so happy. She had her father back, and more, she had her trust in him restored. I would not endanger that, not without proof.

"Well, the prince certainly has faith in you," Allessandra said. One brow was raised, and her lips twitched. I didn't see what was so funny about it.

"I'm just glad the silly slippers fit Maridonna, or whatever her name is," I said, taking up my blue gown and shaking it out vigorously, before slipping it over my head.

"Fit isn't quite the word."

I struggled to get my arms into the sleeves of the gown, and thrust my head through the neck hole with such vigor I tore a seam somewhere under my arm. "What?"

"Oh, she can get her feet into them and shuffle around, certainly. But she had to pack the toes with strips from her chemise. She has such tiny little feet." Allessandra extracted an ivory comb from her pocket. "Now turn around and let me fix this bedraggled mane of yours."

"Did Leonato see?" I asked, wincing when she hit a tangle.

"No, I don't think he or my father noticed a bit. Too busy with other things."

"Her snow-white skin and ruby lips?"

"No, silly girl. I believe the prince was more concerned with you. He spent the greater part of the morning wearing out the floors of this room."

I realized my mouth was open, but I found no words to fill it. Allessandra continued on blithely. "He's a nice fellow, that prince. Not at all what I expect from a noble. Do you know he washed the porridge pot from breakfast? Imagine that. Not at all like the girl. A shame he'll have to marry such a harpy. If you ask me, no kingdom is worth that." She ran the comb through my hair one last time and set to braiding it.

"If my fortune doesn't come true, Papa will be executed," I said at last. "She's a princess, she fits the slippers, well enough at least. He rescued her from dire peril. So he must marry her."

"He must fulfill the prophecy, for certain," Allessandra said. "It's a cursed shame if he must marry her to do so. That's not a happy ending."

"This isn't a fairy tale," I said, jerking away as she tied off the braid. "There's no real magic, why should there be any happily-ever-after?" I swallowed against the tightness in my throat, afraid I was going to burst into tears. I could get through this. I *had* to.

Allessandra regarded me solemnly for a moment, plucking my loose hairs from the teeth of her comb. "I've told enough lies in my life to recognize when something is true."

I shook my head. "That's ridiculous." I turned toward the door. It was cruel of Alle to feed my hope. Better that it shrivel and die and take away this horrible ache in my breast.

Allessandra caught my arm. "Do you love him?"

I didn't answer. I wasn't even sure whether she meant my father or Leonato. It didn't matter. I knew what I had to do. I took a deep breath. "You said you could help us escape the Bloody Captain's soldiers. I don't want to stay here any longer. We're endangering you. We should make our plans and go."

THE PLAN WAS SIMPLE, in theory. We would create a distraction and make for shore under cover of night. Allessandra's Tomas was a spare man with long brown hair and soft eyes. It gave me a queer twist in the chest to watch him showing us around his workshop, for he had that same bubbling enthusiasm Father once had for his craft. The candles Tomas created were as much works of art as any shoes my father made. He showed us how he dipped them in one color of wax after another, then carefully carved fillips and curls along the sides, curving them back or twisting them to display the rainbow of colors within. They were as beautifully elaborate as the palace of Doma, or Zia Rosa's cakes. But Tomas had another craft, also elaborate, also involving light and color. He made fireworks.

This would be our means of diversion. When the southeastern sky was lit with color and crashing with the boom of the explosions, we would slip away to the northwest. Propitiously, the captain had commissioned a display of the best of Tomas's stores for the next night, in celebration of Niccolo's upcoming crowning as king of Sirenza. According to Tomas, the rockets and crackers and such were already in place, in a transport barge down in the south quarter. He need only sneak close enough to set them alight.

Leonato and I waited on the narrow walk along the canal, keeping watch as Tomas rummaged about in the barge, checking his craftings for moisture damage. Leonato stood at the corner where the walk turned to pass under an arch carved with birds. I could make out a thrum of low cooing from that direction; the gilded sign announced it was a dovecote. It was the only sound, other than the lapping of water and the occasional grumble from Tomas when he found a damp wick.

"Fortunata?"

"Yes?" I remained where I was, watching along the canal in the opposite direction.

"Have you ever told a fortune that didn't come true?"

My heart beat faster. Did Leonato know I was a fake? My back was to the prince, so I could not read his expression. I realized I needed to respond. "There's no reason to worry, Your Highness. The fortune is nearly complete. You will fulfill the Edicts."

"But are you s-s-sure Maridonna is the princess?"

That turned me around. Leonato had abandoned his own watch and stood facing me. His golden brows knit together.

"What do you mean? Don't you like her? She's beautiful. Cornsilk hair, ruby lips, skin like cream. She might have stepped from the pages of a fairy tale."

Leonato shook his head abruptly. "No, in the fairy tales I would have fallen in love with her at first s-s-sight. Fortunata, I don't love her. How can I marry her?"

He didn't love her! The words rang through my mind like the glorious trumpets of the Saints. I struggled for words, battling the urge that had risen like a great burning flame in my heart: to tell him not to marry her.

Then I forced myself to recall my mission. I imagined my father, whose only crime had been to believe in his daughter, being led before the headsman's block. "Well, you've only just met. You'll learn to love her. I'm sure you'll be happy together."

It was a lie, and it hurt more than any other I'd told. I could bear to lose Leonato if it was only my heart being torn. But what if Allessandra was right? What if he really did—

No. I could not let myself think that way. I started back to my post.

"Fortunata, I can't marry her, not when I love—"

He fell silent as Tomas scrambled up from the barge. My heartbeat thrummed loud as hoofbeats, but I did not dare ask Leonato to finish his statement.

"All set. Had to repair half a dozen for dampness, but what a show we'll have. You two should head back now. Quick and quiet, and the Saints keep you both. Allessandra will be waiting. I'll stay until the midnight bell. Go on."

We went. I desperately wanted to ask Leonato what he had been about to say, but I could not. My father's fate haunted me, visions of the headsman, black and terrible, his great ax lifted high. Leonato did not seem inclined to finish the conversation. As we hurried back to the eastern quarter, all his attention seemed engaged in some inner world of thought.

When we reached the others, they were in a state. Captain Ribisi glowered like a smoky fire, and lines creased Allessandra's brow, bringing back something of the sharpness I had not seen since our time with Ubaldo. "What's wrong?" I asked her, as she helped me down the slick stone steps to the wooden dock.

"We nearly lost the princess. Fool girl lost herself, in fact, though I minded her to stay close. Father found her nearly under the nose of a guardsman."

Maridonna sat primly in the stern of the rowboat, a dark cloak drawn around her shoulders but cast back so that her fair hair glimmered like an earthbound star. Her nose crinkled slightly as I moved to join her, but she was all smiles and cheer as Leonato followed. He and the captain had made one quick search of the nearby area to make certain we were unwatched. We all remembered the archers from the Perdutto—whoever they were.

I wondered what Maridonna had been about, losing herself. She was a mean-spirited, vicious girl, but she wasn't stupid. The first of the fireworks distracted me from these thoughts. A great shimmering cloud of blue and white lit the sky to the south, chased closely by the tremendous roar. Bursts of red and green and gold followed, casting such brilliance that I began to fear they might reveal us. I heard distant cries of alarm.

"The watch boats are turning south," said Captain Ribisi. "We go now!" Allessandra bent across from the dock, holding out her hand to clasp her father's. Then she set one foot on the side of the boat and helped push it off into the open waters of the Balta.

I HELD MY BREATH as our rowboat bumped up on the sandy banks north of Baltriporto. Thus far we had escaped notice. It seemed a miracle to me. Captain Niccolo might be an evil, slimy scoundrel, but he was good at his job. I was surprised we had not encountered even one watch boat. Then again, the fireworks had been very impressive.

We disembarked, and Captain Ribisi and I dragged the boat under the cover of a willow down along the bank, where a scrubby woodland met the water. Allessandra would retrieve it later. Turning back, I saw Maridonna and Leonato making their way up the slope toward the curve of the north road that looped out from the woods to follow the line of the river. The girl walked with grace and delicacy, yet still contrived to slip and fall against Leonato several times. Eventually he scooped her up in his arms, carrying her over the last bit of grass. I gritted my teeth, unable to suppress a snort of disgust.

Captain Ribisi halted abruptly, head cocked.

"That was me," I said contritely, thinking he must have heard my snort. But the captain drew his hand sharply through the air, silencing me. The distant pop and crackle of the last fireworks echoed across the waters, the only alien sound amid the burble of water, the piping of frogs, and the singing of crickets. Then I heard it: a crunch of wood. Someone was in the scrub above us.

I stood stupidly for a moment, still straining my ears, hoping I was mistaken. Captain Ribisi seized my arm, drawing me down as an arrow hissed through the air. In another heartbeat he was pulling me along the bank, running toward Leonato and calling the alarm. "Ambush! Beware the south bank!"

Leonato took off for the road, still carrying the princess, who was making useless mewling noises. I cursed silently. If she drew that archer's fire with her cries and Leonato was struck, by all the seven Hells, I would make her pay!

I dashed after the prince, desperate to keep him in sight. I could hear tramping behind us now. More arrows hissed through the night air. Leonato disappeared behind a large boulder, and the next moment a shriek filled the air, followed soon after by a grunt, a crash of branches and sticks, and the whinny of a horse.

As the captain and I raced around the boulder, I saw a pair of feet protruding from the dark bushes. A ragged gasp of relief burst from my lips as I saw Leonato attempting to soothe a large black gelding. Maridonna cowered against the boulder. She shrieked again when the captain and I came in sight.

"That's one down, then," said Captain Ribisi, eyeing the feet.

"There are more out there." Leonato, having brought the horse under control, led the beast toward us and thrust the reins into the captain's hands. "Get the princess away from here. Your Highness, please, don't fear. Captain Ribisi will take good care of you." He beckoned to Maridonna.

She rose reluctantly from the boulder. "But will you not come with me?"

"I'll s-s-stay with Fortunata. We'll find another way. It's the princess they're s-s-s—"

"I can't leave you," said Captain Ribisi, as Leonato struggled to speak. But at the captain's words the prince pulled himself straight, took a deep breath, and spoke again without a single falter.

"Yes, Captain, you must. I am your prince. I order you to do this." Leonato's words rang with a strange sort of triumph, despite the situation.

Captain Ribisi hesitated, then jumped up lightly astride the black horse. Maridonna's face twisted with displeasure and fear. She clung to Leonato's arm and opened her mouth, but he whisked her up and handed her to the captain. "No!" she protested, but Captain Ribisi had already wheeled the horse around.

"Saints be with you, my prince," he said. "And you, Prophetess."

Leonato did not even watch them go. He had grabbed tight hold of my hand. "We'll be safer in the woods. It'll be like old times again," he said, with a faint grin.

Brush tangled our path, making it impossible to move without the crackle of twigs. We stumbled through the darkness. I hoped Leonato knew where he was going, for I had lost all sense of direction by that time.

We came out into a bit of a clearing. I saw the paler curve of the road again, off to our right. I was about to suggest we take our chances that way, when a rider plunged out toward us. Leonato thrust me back into the shelter of a laurel bush. As the rider neared, I saw silver glinting in the filtered moonlight: a sword. The prince seized a branch from the forest floor. Ducking under the sweep of the sword, he brought his branch up, catching the rider under the arm.

The sword flew wide. The rider cursed, then grunted

in surprise as Leonato leapt at him. The horse reared. I thought both men would fall. The rider tried to kick free, but Leonato held on grimly. The horse plunged back toward the road, dragging the prince after him.

"Leonato!" I cried, scrambling to follow. Just as I emerged out onto the open road, a figure loomed up across from me. The man gave an evil grin, his eyes narrow and black and pitiless. I opened my mouth, but the scream froze in my throat at the cold certainty that this man would kill me. My last prophecy, and it would be true.

He raised his ax. I could only stare transfixed, my mind screaming at my body to move. I caught a flicker of movement from the woods past the man. His lips slackened, his eyes widened. He pitched forward with a gurgling cry. I looked stupidly down at where he now lay in the road, unmoving, then up again. Leonato must have returned just in time to save me.

But it wasn't the prince who stepped forward from the dark wood. It was Coso. His bright eyes stared at me from under grizzled hair bound back in one of the scarves he and Cristo favored. He held a long blade in his hand, covered to the hilt with blood. Coso grinned, white teeth flashing in the dark, then stooped to wipe the dagger on the back of the dead man's coat.

"Coso? What are you doing here?"

"No thanks, girl? I saved your life." He rose again,

sliding the dagger into a sheath at his side. He crossed his arms.

"But . . .why? You don't care about me."

"Not one jot." He chuckled. "But I do care about the five hundred guilders."

"What five hun—" I stopped abruptly, understanding at last. "My prophecy. You're here to make certain it comes true."

"Of course. Do you suppose Ubaldo would trust a silly chit like you to earn us that coin? You've already made a right mess of things with that stupid prophecy. Witches and magical swords and slippers! Even a real seer couldn't have concocted such a pack of nonsense."

"Ubaldo knows well enough I've no True Sight, that this is all a pack of lies dressed up to look like a prophecy. If only he'd told me what was going on, I could have come up with something better."

"Or simply refused altogether. Enough, girl. I've dealt with this problem for you, but you'd best be on your way now. Just get the boy and his pretty new prize back to Doma. You've done your part. Keep your mouth shut and let us do our job, and you'll have your father back and we'll have our reward. You act smart enough, and Ubaldo might even give you a bit of the coin."

He turned then, and stalked back into the woods. I nearly ran after him to demand that he tell me everything Ubaldo had done, but a noise from down the road drew my attention. Someone was standing there. Leonato.

His face was pale, and drawn so tense I thought at first he must be wounded. He stepped forward stiffly, as if not quite in control of his limbs. "A pack of lies? All of this? All this time? It's been just s-s-some tale you invented, to gain coin?"

I stared back in horror. This couldn't be happening. All I had was Leonato's faith, the brightness in his eyes when he looked at me and believed in me. Now even that was being torn away. I tried to speak, to protest, to find more lies to cover this horrible rending chasm that had suddenly opened at my feet. But the words did not come. My throat clenched so tight I could barely breathe. I nodded.

Leonato bowed his head and turned away from me.

CHAPTER

12

"LEONATO." I FINALLY forced my lips to move, though the word came out as a croak. I reached out for his shoulder, but he pulled away at the slightest touch of my fingers. I snatched back my hand and clutched it to my chest. Coward that I was, I thanked the Saints I could not see his face.

The prince trembled, holding himself perfectly taut and upright, hands stiff at his sides. "You let me believe in this. In myself. But it was nothing, it was lies. And I thought"—he gave a bitter laugh, shaking his head—"I thought I was a hero. But I'm just a lie too. Like Aunt Donata s-s-said."

"You're not!"

"Did I do a s-s-single thing? The s-s-sword? The witch? S-s-saints preserve me, the princess, even? Was that all s-s-some farce? You and your friends laughing at me all the while, the s-s-stupid, s-s-stuttering prince s-s-silly enough to believe in it?" He paced back and forth, running his hands through his loose golden curls.

"The princess is real, as far as I know. I swear by the Saints. I was going to find the first girl who fit the slippers."

Leonato gave a bark of laughter. "As if I can ever believe you again."

Oh, Saints have mercy on me, I had done this to him. I had given him hope and then ripped it away. "You must believe me. You *are* a hero. You saved my life in the Black Wood, and in Sirenza too. You're courageous and kind and just, and you deserve to be king."

"I will not be king by a lie!" He spat out the words, eyes narrowed.

All the coldness filling my breast suddenly frothed up into hot anger. "Then you as good as murder my father. I didn't *want* to do this. I would never have done it, if I'd known how it would end. I would never have risked Papa's life. I would never have hurt you."

"Then why? Why come to this? Why make your life by s-s-selling lies?"

"You have no idea what my life is like," I said bitterly. "You in your palace, with all the food you could wish for, and hot baths, and a gilded roof over your head. Have you ever been hungry, or cold, or wanted for anything you couldn't have?"

Leonato was silent for a long moment, staring at me. "Yes," he said softly, "I have wanted s-s-something I could not have." Then he jerked his head away. He turned back down the road. "But it was a lie as well."

"So. You will have my father killed." Now both the cold fear and the hot anger had left me. I felt like dead dry leaves or an old hollow tree, as if the wind could blow through me. "And your aunt will be queen. She's the one sending these men to kill us, you know," I added dully.

"No." He didn't look back. He untied the leads of the horse he'd secured off the side of the road ahead. "I won't be responsible for that. S-s-saints have mercy, I will not betray your s-s-secret."

"Thank you," I said. It came out as a whisper.

"Don't thank me," he snapped. "I'm doing it for your father, and for Doma. Not for you." He brushed one hand across his face. When he turned to me, his eyes were hard and cold, his mouth in a thin tight line. He thrust the reins into my hands. "Get up. You can ride. My princess is waiting."

THE JOURNEY BACK to Doma was a nightmare. We passed through the same village where Leonato had whirled me around during the feast of Saint Aleppo. I remembered his joy, the way he had seemed to seize all of life. The young man who crossed the square now was stern-faced, cheerless. I had done this. He had made me believe in the joy and wonder of life, and what had I done in return? Destroyed it. Turned it into something sordid and false. I felt like a murderer.

It was far more brutal than simply losing my foolish dream of a future with Leonato. The man I had loved was gone. I tried to cling to my memories, telling myself we had shared something real and true, but with every passing league, they slipped away and turned to dust.

Leonato did not berate me. There were no more recriminations. It was worse than that. He simply ignored me. He was so polite and cool that I almost doubted I had seen that horrible look on his face when he first discovered my lies.

The worst part was watching the prince with Maridonna, after we reunited with her and Captain Ribisi. Before this, he'd treated the princess with a detached courtesy, not even seeming to notice her attempts to secure his attention. Now he attended upon her every word and desire. I watched them with feverish intent, searching for some hint of that old disinterest, a fixed quality to his smile when she sidled up against him, clinging to his arm. But it was more likely my own wishful thinking.

Thank the Saints, at least he had not yet officially asked her to marry him. I supposed he was waiting until the Edicts had been fully verified and authorized. I hoped that when he did, I would be long gone, somewhere I would never hear his name spoken again.

Maridonna did not let this prevent her from embarking on plans for her bridal garb and feast. Even Leonato's determined attention quailed before her stream of chatter about silk and damask, velvet and taffeta, gold goblets and ivory-handled spoons, pastry swans and ten-tiered cakes. Sometimes the prince begged off on such one-sided conversations, to ride ahead and check the condition of the roads. On those occasions, Maridonna settled on me as a surrogate audience, while Captain Ribisi held a position several wagon-lengths back down the trail, watching for any more brigands.

"It must be difficult to make such plans when you have no family to attend the festivities," I said rather sharply one morning, after she had told me for the fifth time about a new pattern of lace she planned to commission for the trim of her bridal undergarments.

She looked puzzled for a moment. "Family? Oh. Yes, well, my darling Leonato will be my family now, of course."

"There are no others left, are there? From your family, the royal house of Sirenza?" I asked. I caught a flicker of something in the princess's lovely face, something that made me struggle again to determine what it was that seemed so familiar.

"Ah, there's my dear prince now," she said in relief.

I looked up to see Leonato astride his bay gelding. He held a bunch of wildflowers in one hand: cornflowers, poppies, yarrow. For the first time in several days, he met my eyes. For a fleeting moment I thought he was going to give the flowers to me; I had to clasp my hands together to keep from reaching for them.

Maridonna had no such compunctions. Her delicate hands darted out to seize the flowers so eagerly that several sprigs fell. She held the posy up to her nose. "Oh, how lovely, my prince!" She glanced at me. "You see how lucky I am, Fortunata, to have the devotion of such a man. Truly there is no woman in the world more blessed by the Saints."

I clenched my fists on Franca's reins and turned my eyes upon her long gray ears. The light breeze caught one of the loose sprigs of yarrow and blew it into the beast's tufted mane.

"We're nearly to Doma. I saw the cathedral s-s-spire from that rise ahead," Leonato said. "We'll reach the city by noon. I will present you to my mother at once, princess. Then the Edicts will be fulfilled. The court will s-s-s—"

Just for a moment, I caught Maridonna's nose crinkling as Leonato fought to speak. "Or I can present myself," Maridonna offered. "Only so you needn't trouble yourself, my darling. In fact, I can speak for you anytime you wish. Though I do hope you'll manage to say your wedding vows for yourself."

Red bloomed in Leonato's cheeks more vivid than the wild poppies. He clamped his lips closed.

"He'll speak his vows as faultlessly as a Saint," I said, glaring at Maridonna.

"Another vision, Prophetess?" said Leonato, harshly. "And I suppose next you'll tell us we're going to live happily ever after?" He looked more grim than Captain Ribisi on his worst day.

"Of course we are, my love," said Maridonna, clutching at Leonato's hand.

They rode forward together, but I did not watch them. I plucked the single stalk of yarrow from Franca's mane and twisted it between my fingers, remembering the night Leonato and I had met in the garden of the inn at Saint Federica's Rest. The night I had fallen in love with him. How I wished I could return to that moment, to somehow make everything right. Was there something I could have said, some way I could have saved my father without hurting Leonato?

I nearly cast the sprig of yarrow aside, down into the dust of the road, along with my hopes and dreams. But I tucked it behind my ear instead, into the coils of my braids. My memories were all I had now.

CHAPTER

13

WE STOPPED A SHORT time later at a small inn on the hill above the city, so that Maridonna might change into the finery she'd purchased earlier in our journey, for her grand entrance. Leonato and Captain Ribisi departed to consult with the complement of guards who would be escorting us the rest of the way. That left me to serve as errand girl to Maridonna, who kept me busy for much of the morning, running to the nearest apothecary for fine soap, to another shop for an assortment of ribbons, even to a sweet-seller for a snack (which she did not share).

It drove hot embers under my skin to help her prepare to wed Leonato. By the time she asked me to run back to the apothecary for the third time, to fetch lavender water for her bath, I was ready to tell her to wash in the pigs' slop basin. Then I saw the lunch tray the innkeeper had just delivered. Beside the plate of dumplings lay a folded square of parchment. Was Maridonna truly forgetful, or did she want me out of her way for some other reason?

"Well? What are you waiting for?" she said. She covered the note with one hand, making the motion casual. But I caught the slight tremor in her fingers.

I forced myself to provide the fawning smile she expected. "I'd be glad to get the lavender water, Princess, but I'm afraid that almond pastry took my last guilder."

She heaved a great sigh, but as I hoped, she also rose and crossed the room to the box containing the coins. I darted forward, snatching up the parchment and scanning it quickly. *Come to the stables. We must speak.* I dropped it back beside the plate as Maridonna returned. She plunked three coins into my hand. "Off you go. Two should be enough. The other is yours to spend. Have one of those pastries yourself." She smiled sweetly. "There's no need to hurry back."

Heart thumping, I departed. I had to find out what Maridonna was up to. Who was she meeting so secretly in the stables? And was she expecting danger? The princess had seemed nervous. Much as I disliked her, I couldn't afford to let my prophecy be jeopardized, not with Father's life still depending on it.

Once outside, I hastened to the long, low building behind the inn. I crept through the kitchen garden and made my way to one end of the stables. I barely breathed, my whole body tensed for the sound of the mysterious person who had summoned Maridonna. I heard nothing but the whiffling of horses and the occasional stamp of a hoof.

Slipping inside, I slunk between the stalls until I found one that was empty. I was just about to enter when footfalls approached. Quickly I ducked inside, shrinking down beside a bale of hay. The tread was too heavy to be Maridonna. It must be the person who had summoned her. A sudden fear seized me. What if she was meeting some secret paramour? Could I conceal such a discovery from Leonato and allow him to marry her?

Worse, what if it was Leonato himself? What if I found myself spying on a lovers' assignation? My heart writhed at the thought.

I had to see who it was. I squinted out through a gap in the boards. All I could see were his legs but it was enough. I would know those scarlet-carved boots anywhere. Captain Niccolo! I felt as if I'd been plunged into an icy river. My greatest enemy stood mere feet away. The man who had held Maridonna prisoner, who had murdered her entire family. Had he summoned her here to kill her too?

The stable doors creaked open again. The footfalls that entered this time were lighter, the patter of slippers. Saints, no! She was walking right into her doom! Maridonna was a vain, selfish girl, but she did not deserve to die. I could at least give her a chance. I sent one last prayer to the Saints, to watch over my father and Leonato when I was gone.

"Run, Princess!" I shrieked as I slammed the door of the stall outward into Niccolo. I had one look at his startled face before he toppled back, cursing. I ran toward Maridonna. She stood wide-eyed, mouth agape. I seized her hand, tugging. "You have to get away. It's the Bloody Captain. He'll kill you!"

Maridonna blinked, then a strange smile twisted her lips. "I hardly think Niccolo would kill his own sister."

The world reeled, the only fixed point Maridonna's beautiful, oddly familiar face. Of course! I was such a fool. I had known she reminded me of someone. Then an arm wrapped around me. Something cold and sharp pressed against my throat. The velvet of Niccolo's doublet brushed the nape of my neck, and his words hissed in my ear.

"Isn't that sweet, Maridonna? The poor girl was trying to save you. I must congratulate you, if you've managed to hide your true nature well enough to provoke such loyalty."

I gave a strangled shriek. "You snake! You harpy!"

"Or perhaps she sees more clearly than I thought," said Niccolo, chuckling.

Maridonna quirked her eyebrows. "The prince likes me. That's all that matters."

"You planned this, you wretch," I hissed, wary of the blade that still rested against my throat. "You set this all up."

"Of course," said Niccolo. "Come, come, Fortunata. Show a bit of good grace. It's thanks to me that your— well, let's just call it imaginative—fortune is coming true. I deserve better than this."

"You deserve to be sliced into a dozen pieces and hung from the walls of the city. And you—" I glared at Maridonna. All the spite and pain that had been stewing inside me for the past two weeks bubbled up in the face of her smirk.

"Don't mind her, she's just jealous," said Maridonna. "She's gone soppy over the prince."

I jerked forward. Niccolo tightened his arm, clamping me closer. "And what of him?" he asked his sister intently. "I trust you've ensured his attentions are not straying?"

Maridonna gave an airy wave. "He mooned over the girl a bit at first. But it was nothing. From what I've seen, he can't bear the sight of her now."

"Then he's asked for your hand?"

Maridonna's smirk wavered.

"Is it the slippers?"

"The slippers fit . . .well enough."

Niccolo's voice grated. "I'm certain I don't need to remind you, dear sister, of how important it is to my plans that we control Doma."

"He's going to ask me. He's just waiting for these ridiculous Edicts to be verified. It's not as if he has any other choice," said Maridonna, talking very quickly. "He's given me sacks of guilders to spend. Anything I want. You should see my gown for my formal presentations. Yards of white silk, and gold rib—"

"Enough." The word was heavy with threats.

Maridonna fell silent. For a strange, short moment, I was reminded of Alle and me, cowed by Ubaldo's rages. I stood painfully taut, like a child waiting for the crash of thunder after that first terrible flash of lightning.

Then Niccolo relaxed. His slow, regular breaths stirred my hair. "So he's a generous lad, is he? And obliging. Good. Perhaps we won't have to remove him."

Chills raced down my back, trembling my legs. The brute was going to kill Leonato! I opened my mouth to cry out, but the blade pricked more closely. I gulped, then hissed the words. "Curse you to the seven Hells if you lay one hand on him. Both of you."

"I've already been cursed by a bishop, Fortunata, as

you may recall. Though I commend your fierceness in defense of a lad who apparently cares nothing for you."

I squeezed my eyes shut for a moment, willing myself not to give in to the misery that roiled in my chest. I could not bear to let Niccolo and his sister mock my pain.

"I won't let you do it," I said at last, when I was certain my voice would not shake.

"And how do you propose to stop me?" said Niccolo. "If Maridonna does not marry the prince, your own father will die. So you don't really have a choice, do you?"

"I—I—" I couldn't think of anything. All I could picture was Father, how much he had trusted me, how it had led him to risk his own life. And Leonato, bright-eyed and glorious, also believing in my lies, also doomed now to die for it. It wasn't fair. They should not have to pay the price. The fault was mine. "I won't let you hurt him," I insisted.

Maridonna looked inquiringly at her brother.

"I'll take care of her," he said, his arm an iron band binding my arms to my sides, nearly crushing my breath now. "You just be sure that stuttering fool finds his tongue long enough to ask you to marry him."

I FOUND MYSELF dragged off, a horse-scented cloth covering my face and clogging my mouth with bits of hay.

With my hands and feet bound, I was slung over the back of a horse and carted away. When I was dragged off again a short time later, the blinding muffle was removed and I found myself in a large room of rough-hewn wood. I staggered back, bumping into something cool and hard. A millstone, dusty and littered with bird droppings. My feet had been untied, but ropes still bound my wrists, and sturdy cord tethered me to an iron ring in the stone.

Niccolo leered at me. "Not the best of accommodations, I know, but it will have to do. Now don't look so glum, girl. I'll be back soon."

"I'd pay a hundred guilders never to see you again," I spat at him.

"Temper, temper. I could easily arrange for you to never see me, or anything else, ever again." He ran one hand over the hilt of his sword.

"What will you do with me?" I asked. The world seemed dim, cheerless, and not just because of the layer of moldering dust that lay across the room. "Why haven't you killed me?"

"Killed you? Fortunata, you don't give yourself enough credit. It would be a crime to kill a girl who can engineer so great a deception as you have. I did my part, of course, but you were doing very well on your own."

His compliments struck me like the jabs of a red-hot

brand. I shook my head, but the words echoed there, taunting me.

"I could put such skills to good use."

"I'll never work for you! I'll never lie like that again. How he must hate—" I clamped my mouth shut as Niccolo chuckled.

"I trust you'll reconsider once I've returned with your beloved father. If you behave, you may even see him before nightfall."

My heart leapt, in spite of all else, before his next words pulled it down again. "He'll be freed once my sister has wed the prince."

I slumped back against the millstone.

"And now I must be off to share in my sister's joy. But don't fear, I won't leave you alone." Niccolo strode to the single door in the far side of the room. He flung it open and Ubaldo slouched in, followed by Coso and Cristo, who were bickering over a dice game. They fell silent at the sight of Niccolo. "You lot, keep a close watch on the girl. She's tricksy, remember that. I'll be back after dark."

Ubaldo smiled ingratiatingly. "Of course, Captain. You can rely on us, as you always have." He cleared his throat. "And will . . . that is, will you have my reward when you come back? The girl's fortune came true, didn't it?"

"You will get your reward, Ubaldo," said Niccolo, not bothering to stop. I caught a quiet grumble from Cristo, a glower from Coso at Ubaldo's back. They hadn't liked Ubaldo's talk of "his" reward, had they? It was the slightest thread, but I clutched at it. I had built fortunes on a single scar, a smile, a word. Could I construct an escape from a grumble?

I settled back against the millstone, trying to look meek. Ubaldo spent a long, tedious time haranguing me for my extravagant fortune. I bent my head, shivering, but it wasn't Ubaldo's words that shook me. Visions of Leonato swam before my eyes. The prince and Maridonna speaking vows in a grand cathedral. Niccolo springing out at him, arcing a sharp blade at his breast. Or would Maridonna do it herself? I saw her offering him a bridal cup of poisoned wine, him raising it to his lips, prepared to drink the bitter draught. And it was all because of me. I slumped, banging my forehead against my knees.

But I could not give up now, not when there was still a chance I could set things right. Taking long, deep breaths, I concentrated on my three captors, all senses pricked for any tidbits I could turn to my advantage.

Coso and Cristo had returned to their dice game, hunkered down not far from the millstone. Ubaldo had lost interest in yelling at me and now stood to one side of the room, sending one dagger after another into a post a few feet away. I shivered with each thud, sensing how easily he might have sent one of those blades flying into me. I suspected that was his intention.

If I could distract them long enough to grab one of those daggers, I could cut my bonds and run. They had horses tethered outside—I could hear them. And we must not be far from Doma, considering how quickly we'd gotten here. With the amount of primping Maridonna had planned, she and the others might not even have left the inn yet.

Ubaldo stomped forward to collect his half-dozen daggers. I hunched, attempting to look cowed. If he thought I was afraid, he was sure to continue. He was that sort of man. He gave me an evil grin as he returned to his position and began anew.

I turned my attention to Coso and Cristo. I just needed the right opening. A short while later, I had it. Cristo grimaced after Coso won yet another game. "That's it. I won't risk any more. Need to keep my belly full." He jerked a thumb at Ubaldo, lowering his voice. "Who knows what crumbs he'll be giving us."

"Watch yourself," said Coso, with a wary look at Ubaldo, who was still tossing his daggers.

"You're right," I said, pitching my voice low. "You're not going to see a single coin of the reward."

Both men looked at me. Coso frowned, but Cristo blinked and licked his lips nervously. "What would you know?" said Coso.

"I see many things—" I began.

Coso grunted. "We know your prophecies are all a fat lot of dross."

"Not all of them," Cristo countered, poking the older man's shoulder. "Remember? We didn't do anything to make that part about—"

"That doesn't matter. We had a deal. We get a share."

"The way you always got a share of the wine? Or the nut cakes?" I paused, letting that sink in. Ubaldo stomped forward to collect his daggers once more. I huddled against the millstone, waiting for the thunk of metal into wood to resume.

Thunk. I took a deep breath. Now it was time for my gambit. It was a risk, but one I would have to take. "If that's so, where are your gold chains?" The two of them hadn't been there to see Ubaldo steal Father's chain of mastery from me, and I was betting that the selfish brute had kept it hidden from them ever since.

"Gold chains?" repeated Cristo.

"Ubaldo has one," I said. "It was a gift from the Bloody Captain. The first of many, but you won't be seeing a single glint of gold."

The two men looked at each other. *Thunk. Thunk.*

Ubaldo's daggers flew into the wood. Now, I thought, willing Coso and Cristo to act.

Ubaldo still held a dagger in each hand when Cristo stood and approached him. "So, Ubaldo," he said, "I hear the Bloody Captain's been generous. And when were you planning to give us our share?"

Ubaldo glowered at the younger man. "What are you spouting now? What share?" He raised his hand, ready to fling another dagger.

I held my breath at the flash of gold from his collar. Thank the Saints. He was wearing it.

"It's true!" Cristo seized Ubaldo's shirt, tugging it. "The gold chain!"

"Hands off!" roared Ubaldo, raising the dagger. Coso leapt forward, drawing a blade of his own. Suddenly all three of them were shouting. It was time to take my chance.

I lunged for the post, straining at the very end of my tether to reach one of the daggers. The hilt slid against my sweaty palms. It was hard to maneuver it with my bound hands.

Ubaldo was cursing, Cristo yelling. I heard thuds, grunts, staggering footsteps. I ignored them. If I did not get free now, all would be lost. At last the ropes parted. I wrenched my wrists free and ran.

I burst out the door, panting. Three horses were

picketed outside. I loosed the two mares and threw myself onto the gelding, praying he would behave. I could hear Ubaldo shouting as I galloped away, but I was more terrified of what I might discover when I reached the city. Leonato, married already to a woman who would murder him or make him her brother's puppet. Please, I prayed, let me get there in time to stop it.

CHAPTER

14

"LET ME IN!" I demanded of the guard before the doors that led to the great hall. "I have to see the prince. I know he's in there." I tried to push past. The guard shoved me back. I wanted to weep from the frustration and fear coursing through me.

Suddenly the doors opened and Captain Ribisi slipped through. He considered me, frowning. "Prophetess. What are you doing here? Princess Maridonna said you were unwell."

"She lied. Please, Captain, you must let me in. Leonato's life is in danger. She's not who she said. Maridonna is the Bloody Captain's sister!"

Captain Ribisi stared at me a moment. Then he motioned the guard aside and opened the doors into the great hall.

Leonato and Maridonna were standing at the far end of the room, on the dais before the queen and the empty throne. I raced toward them, all noise dimming but for the clatter of my own running feet. "Stop!" I shouted.

Leonato and Maridonna turned around. Every eye was upon me. This was it. I was about to destroy everything I had worked so hard for. But I had to save Leonato.

"She's not a princess," I cried. "She's the Bloody Captain's sister. It's all a trick to gain control of Doma. The fortune was a lie." I raised my eyes to Leonato, hoping he would hear the truth of my words now. "They're going to use you, or kill you. I know you can't forgive me, but please, by all the Saints, don't marry her!"

The words left me empty, yet at the same time a triumphant vigor buzzed through my limbs. It was done.

"Yes, Maridonna is my sister," said Niccolo. "But she is also, quite lawfully, a princess."

He sauntered forward until he stood an arm's length from me. A hum of excitement coursed through the onlookers. They drew back, creating a pool of empty space around us. That shiver of steel behind me must mean Captain Ribisi had drawn his sword. But no one else moved, except Niccolo, who reached up, pulling off his ostentatiously large hat to reveal the gleam of a golden crown.

"What madness is this?" demanded the queen.

"I am king of Sirenza, you see. I've received the

blessing of the priests and had my name recorded in the great book of sovereigns."

"You took the crown by force," Leonato said. A thrill went through me. He was fighting back. Did he believe me? Another, more desperate thought chased the first. Did he forgive me?

"Ah, yes, but according to the quite sensible laws of Sirenza, that is what gives me the right of kingship. Anyone who defeats the current monarch and forces him to yield the crown is entitled to rule. So, I am king, and Maridonna, as my sister, is princess."

"But then I didn't rescue her," said Leonato. "Sh-sh-she was never in any peril."

"The archers at the tower were trying to kill me," said Maridonna at once. "And the thugs on the riverbank. Those weren't my brother's soldiers."

"No," said Niccolo. "There was another force seeking my sister's death." He shot a look at Princess Donata, who was lurking to one side of the dais. "Someone who didn't want to see this prophecy come to pass."

"You saved me from them, my prince." Maridonna leaned toward Leonato.

"So there you have it," said Niccolo. "All your Edicts are met. Doma gains a king and my sister becomes queen. And of course our two lands will share in peace and prosperity."

"Leonato?" asked the queen. The prince stood stiffly.

He glanced once toward his aunt, then at Maridonna, then at his own fists, as if he might squeeze the answer to his dilemma out of thin air. I understood. Two bad choices felt like no choice at all. And it was my own fortune that bound him now.

The queen spoke again. "Princess Maridonna does fulfill the prophecy, Leonato. You rescued her. She wears your grandmother's slippers. The Edicts are satisfied. You can be king, as you are meant to be."

"No," I began. "She—"

Niccolo seized my shoulder, wrenching me toward him. "Not another word," he hissed.

"The slippers don't fit!" I shouted and brought my heel down on his foot. He stumbled, but didn't release me. I punched at him wildly; my fist connected with smooth metal, edged with points. The crown. I grasped it as we tumbled to the floor.

I scrambled to get free. Niccolo sprang upright, lithe as a cat, his rapier drawn. "You scheming little chit," he spat. I crouched, panting.

Niccolo jabbed the blade at me. The world seemed to have slowed. I saw the open mouth of the queen as she called something, Captain Ribisi jumping forward, the guards not far behind. Leonato was running toward me, a sword in his hand, his lips parted too. Calling my name, I thought, and that gave me courage. But it was all too slow to save me.

Then, suddenly, my father was there, pounding on Niccolo with his fists. Niccolo jerked back with a furious oath. He swept a powerful backhand blow at my father, knocking him square in the face. Something flew aside with a tinkle of breaking glass. Father fell back.

"Papa!" I screamed, but Niccolo stabbed at me again.

The rapier plunged at my chest. In desperation I held up the only thing in my hands: the crown. Metal shrieked against metal. The blade had caught in the ornate gold-work. I wrenched the crown like a wheel, torquing the weapon so that it flew from Niccolo's grasp. He staggered forward, losing his balance this time.

I stooped to recover the rapier and turned to face him, holding the blade outstretched. He stared at me in amazement, as if he did not understand what had just happened.

"Yield," I said, jabbing the weapon in the air to emphasize my point. Niccolo shook his head in disbelief, then dropped his head into his hands. His shoulders quivered. He was laughing, but it was a hollow, bitter laugh. I wondered if he had gone mad. He said, past the chuckles, "I yield. The crown is yours."

Three guards darted forward. Niccolo made no protest as they pulled him away to join his sister. I saw that the queen now held one of the golden slippers, along with a wad of cloth apparently extracted from the toe.

"Papa?" I asked, helping my father back to his feet. He blinked and squinted. His spectacles were gone. A scattering of glass and twisted wire upon the floor was all that remained of them.

"Well enough, Nata, well enough."

"Oh, Papa, I'm so glad you're all right. I've missed you so." I hugged him fiercely. His rough, strong fingers stroked my hair.

He pulled back to look me over again, smiling. "You've grown, I think. Even more like your mother, now. You've done well, my dear girl, very well."

"Oh, Papa, no, I've made a terrible mess of everything—"

My words were cut off as Leonato caught me in his arms, crushing me to him. "S-s-saints be praised! Are you s-safe?"

I gripped him tight, as if he were pulling me from the depths of some dark chasm. I drew a deep breath, then the words rushed out. "I'm sorry, truly. I didn't know about Ubaldo's plan. Please, by all the Saints, by my mother's spirit, I swear it. I just wanted to save my father. And for you to be king. That's the truth. Please forgive me."

"I believe you," he said gently. "I forgive you." He brushed back the locks of hair that had pulled loose from my braids. "I love you." For a breathless moment, I thought he would kiss me.

I wanted nothing more than to return that embrace, to

say what was in my own heart. But I knew it was not over. I gently pulled away from Leonato. I tried to disengage his hand from my own, but he did not release me. Well, perhaps it would give me courage. I turned to the queen.

"Your Highness, my fortune has not come to pass."

"Fortunata, what are you doing?" said Leonato, his grip tightening. I did not look at him, but took a deep breath and plunged onward. "Please, I beg you for mercy. My father is innocent. If you must punish someone, take me. I'm the one who told the false fortune. If anyone must die for that, let it be me."

"No!" Leonato's cry shivered through the great hall, which had grown suddenly silent.

"I made it all up. It was a lie," I said. I couldn't look at my father, but I heard him protesting, trying to reach me.

"I'm sorry, my nephew," said a cold voice. Princess Donata now stood in the center of the dais, one hand resting on the back of the empty throne. "It must be a great shock to learn how you have been deceived. To learn that your victories were hollow, your triumphs undeserved, thanks to this girl and her cohorts. But you must confront the truth. Doma needs a true sovereign, someone with the real strength to lead our people."

"No. You will not be queen, Aunt," Leonato said firmly. "I will fulfill the Edicts. The prophecy is true." He clenched my fingers.

"It's not—" I began.

"You're the princess." Leonato reached for my other hand, which still held the crown. He pulled my wrist up, so that the whole room might see. "You took this from the king of S-s-sirenza. That makes you the ruler of that city. Princess. Well, queen, actually, but that sh-sh-should be good enough."

Excitement stirred through the crowd. My father stood taut and alert, peering at me and the prince. Princess Donata remained beside the throne, her long fingernails digging into the wood.

Leonato marched toward his mother, pulling me along. "Mother, may I have that s-slipper?"

The queen looked surprised to discover it was still in her hand. Leonato took it from her, then hastened to where the soldiers held Niccolo and Maridonna. Nimbly he caught Maridonna's foot as she tried to kick him and slipped off the other gold shoe.

He knelt before the dais and placed the gold slippers on the floor. I stood stupidly, staring at them, at him, at the gold crown I still clutched. Leonato had to kneel at my feet and loosen the ties of my own bumblebee boots to rouse me from this stupor. It was too fabulous to be true. I looked for my father.

"Believe in it, Nata. Go on." He was squinting so tightly to see me his eyes were mere slits, but he smiled broadly. My heart seemed to be beating quicker than a bird's wings.

Holding my breath, I slid first one, then the other foot into the golden slippers.

"They fit!" Leonato proclaimed. He spun me around; the world became a dizzying blur and he was the center of it.

Then a terrible shriek filled my ears. Princess Donata still stood beside the throne, one hand clutching it. Her lips curled back to show a mouthful of sharp white teeth. From a fold in her dark skirts, she pulled a long silver dagger. With a wordless scream, she launched herself at Leonato. She hung in the air, almost as if she were truly flying. I screamed too, seeing what she intended. I threw myself forward.

I thudded into Donata, cracking my forehead as sharply as if I'd hit a stone wall. The dagger skittered away, but Donata's viselike fingers clutched my neck. She shook me, choking my breath. My chest tightened, and a buzzing grayness flickered at the edges of my mind. My hair tumbled loose, the braids whipped past my face as she shook me again.

Then she shrieked, releasing me so abruptly I fell to the floor. "No, it's not possible. How? How did you know?" She screamed again, casting something away from her as if it were burning.

It was the sprig of yarrow I had tucked in my hair—had it only been that morning? I recalled Grimelda's words. *Yarrow has a baleful effect on demons.*

Donata staggered back. Her beautiful face was now terrible, pure white with violent red streaks across her cheeks. The lines that had been smooth and lovely were now harsh and stark as a skull. She stood hunched, her fingers crooked like the talons of an eagle. She reached out one hand, trying to rake me with those long nails. Then she collapsed, her breaths coming ragged and guttural.

The guards who carried her away did so warily, for she writhed and twitched. A moment later, she was gone. I let out my breath, unable to take in all that had happened, unable to concentrate on anything other than Leonato running to my side. "I'm all right," I said as he seized my hands. All around us chatter rose from the crowd of onlookers.

Then Leonato pulled me close and kissed me. And suddenly all the clamor was like the distant murmur of the sea. All I knew was the beating of my heart, and of Leonato's pressed close beside it.

I don't know how long it lasted, but when he pulled away, flushed, eyes shining, I murmured, "Don't stop."

"I wouldn't," he said softly, his green eyes catching the light like a forest pool. "But there's something I wanted to ask. Princess Fortunata, will you marry me?"

"Yes," I said, "of course."

THANKFULLY, THE QUEEN and court approved our interpretation of the prophecy: Leonato would be the next king of Doma, enabling the queen to retire from her regency. This prospect brought considerable joy to both the queen and Captain Ribisi. Seeing the pair of them standing arm in arm, I blushed to remember my past suspicions of the man. Father gave the engagement his blessing as well, but made us promise to delay our vows until he'd crafted a new pair of shoes for me to wear at the wedding. Thinking of the past monstrosities my father had produced, I made Leonato swear he wouldn't laugh when we arrived to see the newest creations. It didn't matter what shoes I wore, I told myself. I had Leonato. Though I did cherish a faint hope that they would at least not be ruffled and pink like the sausage boots I had once sold Niccolo.

"Nata, Nata!" called my father, bustling out from the workshop Leonato had appointed for his use. His new spectacles made him look even more owlish. He hurried toward us, holding out a pair of shoes.

They were beautiful. A pale blue, like cornflowers, but deeper and more pure. Silver braiding edged each graceful curve; even the laces ended in delicate silver tassels. They were the most lovely pair of shoes I had ever seen. "Do you like them?"

"They're beautiful!" said Leonato. "And just the color of your eyes, Fortunata."

I reached out to take one gently. I felt as if it might vanish in a puff, like the head of a dandelion. But I could feel the smooth leather, the cording of the braid, the brush of the tassels.

"But, how? Papa, how?"

"The fairies, they came back. See, there!" Father gestured proudly to the glittering silver tools arrayed on the heavy worktable at the center of the room.

I took up one of the awls, turning it this way and that in the clear sunlight. It was perfectly clean. "You did this," I said, turning on Leonato as soon as my father had returned to puttering with his shelf of dyes.

"Not I," Leonato protested mildly. "It must have been magic, as your father s-s-said. Fairies."

"I don't believe in fairies," I began. But I stopped then, for I caught sight of something glittering near the foot of the table, where a shaft of sunlight laid a band of gold across the floor. I bent down to look, disbelieving. I swept my finger over the floor, and it came away covered in a fine shimmering powder, opalescent as mother-of-pearl and brighter than diamonds.

"What's this?"

"Fairy dust?" suggested Leonato.

I shot him a suspicious look. "Did you do this too?"

He was smiling. "I told you, it must be magic. Even if you don't believe in it, that doesn't mean it's not there."

"Hmph. Next you'll be telling me we're going to live happily ever after."

"You're the fortune-teller, not I," he said, coming closer to slip his hands around my waist.

"I suppose the last one did come out well enough, in the end," I admitted, covering his hands with mine. His curling hair brushed my cheek, soft as a kiss. "All right then, we will live happily ever after."

Leonato never did admit to cleaning Father's shoe-making tools, nor to spreading the glittering dust. I did not ask again. Perhaps I had started to believe again in magic, or perhaps in love. Or perhaps they were the same thing.

ACKNOWLEDGMENTS

This book could not have been written without the support of those who believed in me even when I didn't believe in myself. Thanks to Robert Fagan, Paul, Cynthia and David Van Der Werf, Maureen Drouin and Mathew Scease, and all my friends and family.

I've been blessed to work with a crew of amazing people on this book.

My wonderful agent, Shawna McCarthy, who plucked Fortunata out of obscurity and found her a home. Reka Simonsen, my brillant editor, who generously shared her wisdom and insights to make my story the best it could be. Ana Deboo, George Wen, April Ward, and Jason Reigal who expertly turned my words into a real book.

I also owe a huge debt of thanks to my fellow writers. Thanks to Geoff Bottone, Allison Corbett, and Kim Sward for their feedback on early drafts. Thank you to Roger Alix-Gaudreau, Melissa Caruso, Jen Connolly, John J. Corbett III, Megan Crewe, and Elizabeth Lee for much-needed encouragement over the years.